I0653020

The Dance of the Shadows

Maria Gabriela Madrid

The Dance of the Shadows
All Rights Reserved
© 2025, Maria Gabriela Madrid
Pukiyari Editores

Reproduction of this book, in whole or in part, is strictly prohibited. This book may not be reproduced, transmitted, copied, or stored, in whole or in part, by any means or form, including graphic, electronic, or mechanical, without the express written permission of the author, except for brief quotations used in articles and written reviews about the book.

ISBN: 978-1-63065-170-1

To my mom Olga Madrid Maya de Madrid, my husband Augusto Parra, my daughter Alejandra Parra Madrid, my sisters Maria Eugenia Madrid and Tatiana Madrid Castillo who always supported my passion for literature and the creation of all future endeavors.

To Lorena Diaz Barrera and Deborath Lombardi Scalise, for their encouragement to pursue this book.

To Jody Moreen, who made possible the compilation of this book.

To all those reflected in my short stories.

To the mystery of the shadows that surround the dreams.

Table of Contents

Maria Gabriela Madrid

Prologue

Maria Gabriela Madrid's short stories are representatives of what is called bio-fiction (a combination of fiction and biography, not necessarily about the personal life of the author), finding in most of the stories descriptions based on subtle warps that, without neglecting the literary level, lead to surprising endings that impact and captivate the reader.

These stories are told with the economy of language that border on literary minimalism. The author uses humor and irony, in the sense of distancing herself. It's about fiction interwoven with traces of everyday reality and imagination, clearly marking the dividing line between reality and the purest literary fiction in which the characters that populate the stories develop, resulting in a discursive ludic universe where it formal literary and expressed reality intermingle, offering the reader a unique product in its creative originality.

Maintaining a certain thematic unity, Maria Gabriela Madrid's work is structured around a credible fiction, without displays of erudition, with certain fantastic touches, although always bound by the essential verisimilitude, which facilitates the reader's understanding of the historical and social framework of the centuries.

Although consistent with the short story formula of beginning, middle and end, these stories demonstrate bold, imaginative leaps toward a narrative situated in the millennium that has just begun. The author's cosmopolitan imagery expands toward the collective in

The Dance of the Shadows

stories such as "Black and White" "Mamoon" and "Woman of the 21st Century," demonstrate the capacity for psychological inquiry and structural sufficiency that characterizes Maria Gabriela Madrid's narrative approach to contemporary Latin American literature.

The Editors
Circle of Writers of Venezuela

Maria Gabriela Madrid

Comments

Comments by Carmen Cristina Wolf
(Poet and President of the
Writers' Circle of Venezuela)

The book "Entre los Surcos del Recuerdo" consists of twenty-three stories written between 2002 and 2006 in North Carolina and New York City, according to its author, Maria Gabriela Madrid. It was published by the Circle of Writers of Venezuela in 2008 and features a Salvador Dali work on the cover entitled "The Persistence of Memory." An intelligent synthesis of verisimilitude and fantastical events laden with mystery, it reveals an insightful exploration of passions through the psychology of the characters, drawn accurately and concisely. With the same ease, it addresses central themes, delving into the fears and insecurities of the psyche that have been addressed since Greek Tragedy, as well as highly current and controversial issues, such as the deterioration of the planet, slavery, and tyranny. It addresses jealousy, envy, obsessions, heartbreak, persecution for religious reasons, and the stigma of prejudice. It could be said that she would have become a good disciple of Horacio Quiroga, who recommends writing with simple words, without excessive adjectives, leading the characters firmly to the end without the writer being distracted from that path traced with tedious and unnecessary descriptions.

The author exhibits an absolute disregard for what friends, acquaintances and critics might think about her writing. And according to Venezuelan writer Heberto Gamero, stories should be "a perfect, small, and precise sculpture." I observe that Maria Gabriela achieves this goal in her craft as a storyteller. Maria Gabriela's stories do not indulge in descriptions that take us out of the tension, and when the reader begins to read, it's as if they're climbing a trapeze rope. In other words, she holds the reader's attention, and they cannot stop in the middle of the void. They must reach the end.

Even though MGM uses the traditional structure of introduction, middle, and end, the characters often move into other settings and break this common thread by using surrealist devices without losing the thematic unity.

For poets like me, immersing myself in the short story is a fascinating universe. Since I began reading Chekhov, Poe, Horacio Quiroga, Maupassant, Onetti, and re-reading Borges with a new, inquisitive eye, I have taken immense pleasure in reading this literary genre and I find in Maria Gabriela's book the application of the secrets of the masters, as I mentioned earlier. She does not use unnecessary adjectives, and she does not distract the character with secondary matters. She writes with clarity. She does not describe the psychic world of the characters; they reveal themselves through their thoughts and actions.

Just as we welcome a new being when a mother gives birth, in the same way we share the joy of this new child of Maria Gabriela, conceived through the meticulous and painstaking work of this young Venezuelan author.

Words spoken by Carmen Cristina Wolf on July 16, 2009, at the book launch of "Entre los Surcos del Recuerdo" at El Buscon bookstore, Trasnocho Cultural in Caracas, Venezuela.

Comments by Isabel Cecilia Gonzales Molina (Writer and Director of Foreign Affairs for the Writers' Circle of Venezuela)

A few days ago, Michael Jackson died. The news immediately became the center of attention, which upset our president because, for him, it was more important that the situation in Honduras be covered. That got me thinking: Which news was more important? Both are.

Freedom of expression doesn't mean the imposition of opinions, but rather the right of everyone to have an opinion and to be able to express it. But even more important is that each of us can choose to be informed in a timely manner about what interests us. We can change the channel, the station, buy this or that newspaper, even disconnect. No one should tell us what is most important, much less imposing a single vision, because that is the seed of fanaticism, the gateway of darkness.

Maria Gabriela is a writer who has developed this theme in many of her stories. A great example is "Black and White", in which the people are divided into two sides: "The followers of the Oracle of Ifa and those of the Catholic religion." We see how we cover ourselves with fear, and it is this fear that leads us to the destruction of others, to their annihilation and our own.

This also happens in "The Three Snakes" where the protagonist flees trying to save herself from fanaticism, only to discover that fanaticism lives within her, that she is not only a victim of it but accepts it, shares it, multiplies it, and gives it new life.

Lately, we act as if we are afraid of the plurality of though and cling to familiar spaces, whether they work or not. We pretend to live in big cities, immersed in small spaces, behind our walls and barriers. This is what happens in Maria Gabriela's stories, in which her characters wander through a town, that a small hell that's a big hell, the one we carry inside us since birth, no matter whether we live in New York, Raleigh, or Paris. You take your family, your traditions, your beliefs with you everywhere. You take your prejudices with you. You don't change; You are always the same, the one we learned to be.

Most of Maria Gabriela's characters represent failed beings who once tried to be different. Characters who once resolved not to repeat themselves but lacked the strength or courage to change. Change requires true will, real desire, and effort.

Maria Gabriela aims to show us how our society has become empty, how the couple vanishes in marriage when two people are united for the sole reason of not having anyone else. The author questions us, tacitly asks us if we are like them, if we love in pieces, if we abandon, if we have children to fulfill, if what matters to us is appearance, the image of the happy couple, the image of the perfect mother, the image of the 21st century woman, the one who only seeks to show off.

"So, what happened to the enrichment of the intellect that was so proclaimed? To search for one's own identity?"

It happened, Maria Gabriela, it happened, that without realizing it, we stopped searching. That is what you want to convey to us. Your message is direct and effective. We do not want to accept it, but we have failed as a society. The 21st century, for those of us who waited for it, was a dream of progress that we failed to grasp. The hippies abandoned the streets and moved to Wall Street, the feminists found a husband a dedicated themselves to being the same mother they criticized, the environmentalists signed agreements in millions of papers, the politicians divided up the states while citizens were more interested in going out to shop. We returned to war, we returned to pain, we returned to loneliness, we returned to what we recognized as wrong, but that is so known and familiar to us, that it seems the only way to live.

Your stories reminded us of every image and in every story that we become those we didn't want to be, but also, they invite us to meditate on this, to look in the mirror, to realize that it is not too late yet. It is never too late to do the right thing, it is never too late to be different, it is never too late for love, but we must act, we must change, we must dare to live.

Your stories remind us in every image and every story that we became those we didn't want to be, but they also invite us to meditate on this, to look at ourselves in the mirror, to realize that it is not too late yet.

It is never too late to do the right thing, it is never too late to be different, it is never too late for love, but we must act, we must change, we must dare to live.

*This book is a compilation of stories that make up the
book "Entre los Surcos del Recuerdo"
and new stories*

The Dance of the Shadows

Empty Screen

The moments of excitement and pride are behind. With two novels published and hundreds of unfinished stories, Laura is under pressure to produce more. Three years have gone by, letters from her agent, and phone calls echoing in her head like the daily chimes of the cathedral across the street. Since living in the United States, she has had to move several times, this time to an apartment where the passage of time rings and resonates, bouncing off her temples every fifteen minutes, half an hour, three-quarters of an hour, BANG! And each hour is marked by the bell tower, a witness to her lack of concentration and inability to connect her thoughts, loose images that begin the writing process, constructing characters, situations, dreams, desires, and fears to ultimately shape her stories.

Distraught, she goes out into the street to recharge with the energy of the passersby. Anonymous beings in skirts, shorts, pants, miniskirts, children, young people, and old people with iPods and iPhones; no one speaks to anyone, just men in dark suits mumbling about what they must do, or perhaps talking to a colleague on the new devices attached to their ears, hidden by their hair, as if it were an epidemic. So many crazy people talking to themselves on the streets of New York!

Upon returning home, she tries to type at her keyboard, but the intrusive chimes interrupt her, leaving her lost in front of the blank screen. It is already four o'clock, and: bang! bang! bang! bang! Desperate, she puts her hands to her temples and screams, screams, and screams.

Federico once told her that for occasions like this, the best thing is the scream therapy. Of course, she must do it locked in the bathroom to avoid disturbing her neighbors.

Slumped on the couch, she comes out of trance when she hears the increasingly loud knocking on the door.

"Are you okay, Mrs. Laura? Can I help you with anything?"

"Everything is fine," she replies in a hoarse voice, her throat sore from screaming so much.

"Are you sure? I can't hear you well! Why don't you open the door?"

Adjusting her clothes, she turns the brass handle and, showing half her face, tells her everything is under control.

Frustrated, she decides to make tea and cookies which will calm her and give her the strength to continue. It is six in the evening. She goes out onto the balcony, tea in hand, and while she watches the sunset, fascinated, she remembers that Federico is about to arrive, and dinner is not ready. Not in the mood to cook, she takes out a whitish chicken, ready to be baked. Seeking an exotic flavor, she rubs it with spices brought from India.

She remembers her loved ones, those living and those who have passed away. She remembers family gatherings, the smell of wet earth, the evening crickets' songs, the lizards flitting across the ceiling beams. Absentminded, she forgets to put the chicken in the oven.

Thinking it's ready and ready to slice it, she leaves it marinating in the glass container. She plugs in the knife and continues dreaming of the life she left behind.

Searching for strategies to overcome the block that prevents her from writing, Laura comes across the image of her aunt Elena, elegant, made up, wearing a long dress and high heels, who, circling the table, lights three candles and invokes her favorite writers in a prayer. Then, with the candles lit, she sits down and, with the muses in hand, lets the muses take over her being. Like Elena, the artists in the family have managed to overcome their block. Aunt Irene, now deceased, wrote children's stories, Aunt Mariela, a writer, sees her books transcending borders. While Aunt Nora strings together colorful beads and precious stones in front of her silver and crystal sculptures.

Leaving her memories aside, she takes a suitcase out of the closet, puts in a few changes of clothes, and leaves it in the main living room.

Hungry, she remembers she hasn't had dinner. Seeing the light flickering, she presses the answering machine button and hears Federico's voice, telling her that he is on his way. Still thinking about her upcoming novel, she holds the marinated chicken, still half-frozen, in one hand, while, with the other, she turns on the knife. First, second, third slice, and a fourth is left half-cut because the piece of ice caused the electric knife to slip and quickly slice off a large part of her left forearm. Gushes of blood run with the fury of fire, freeing Laura from her block and anticipating the creation of characters, situations, dreams, desires, and fears. Neither the blood, nor the fragments of skin, nor the intense pain will change the placidity of her face. She no longer has a block and is only waiting for the moment to begin her novel.

She knows it will be realistic with certain fantastical touches and will fall within the literary genre of bio fiction. It will tell the family's story, from the first relative to arrive in Venezuela, the one who came from Spain, on the second ship after the conquest. She knows the investigation will be long and will interweave past generations with new ones.

Seeing Laura injured, Federico, horrified, feels his legs tremble, he feels like he's going to faint, but gathering his strength, he grabs the dishcloth, rolls it up, and ties it around her upper forearm, trying to use the tourniquet to stem the blood and save the hand she's writing with. Hurriedly, he calls emergency services and carries her to the doorway.

The ambulance siren announces that it is nearing her destination, its sound mingling with the bells; while Laura, semi-conscious, imagines Aunt Elena, candles lit, writing in solitude. Bathed in blood, lying on the stretcher, Laura, exhausted, looks at Federico, and the suitcase. The chimes that still echo in her mind remind her that the time has come to escape.

Dormant Memories

"I'll summarize what you said. Every time you try to go shopping, you feel your heart race, and then you feel a choking sensation that makes it hard to breathe."

"Yes, and the last thing I told you is also about the itchy feeling when I work on my sculptures. I don't know what else to do; I can't run errands, and now my job is compromised."

"I'll work on this information but also write down what you think might have happened inside the store."

"But, you know, I don't remember anything at all."

"It's okay, just write down whatever comes to mind. Let the ink flow."

"Is that all?"

"Yes, and I'll see you next Tuesday."

Grabbing my purse, I walked away from the building and walked several blocks downhill.

Spring was in full bloom, and the following days were truly intense. Writing down whatever came to mind put a lot of stress on me, as it reminded me of the importance of uncovering the truth. I tried to write, but nothing came, until one night I went to sleep and had one of the most vivid dreams I've ever had.

It was Saturday morning, and my mom, rushing to get ready, quickly tied my hair into a long ponytail. Then she grabbed a light blue T-shirt and a pair of jeans. That morning, she wanted to get to the store early, before everyone else, because she wanted to shop without anyone around. Practically first in line, she took my hand and ran into the store with me. I was a four-year-old girl, and while she browsed the shelves, I played hide-and-seek. Sneaking under a dress whose fabric depicted a plain of sunflowers, I pretended I was in a meadow picking flowers, while my distraught mother called my name. I played for a while, laughing as I hid under different types of clothing. For minutes, perhaps for her I was hiding nearby, but I wasn't. I wanted to win, and I hid under a pair of blue pants where I pretended to swim in an ocean without fish, just the clear water and me. But suddenly, a shark disguised as a man pulled my arm and dragged me out of my hiding place. Frightened, I kicked him and tried to scream, but his sweaty hand covered my mouth. I was terrified, and my eyes screamed with terror, so I thrashed around and tried to get someone to see what was happening, but unfortunately, people were too busy looking at clothes to notice what was happening around them. Quickly, while I was crying silently, the man carried me out of the store and ran down the street until we reached a brick building. Still, he carried me upstairs, and once inside the apartment, he locked me in for hours in a dark, damp room. The roof had a leak, and the constant sound of falling water made me feel dizzy for a moment. The room had previously been a nursery, so there was mud everywhere. Afraid and alone, I sat in a corner, stopped crying, and pretended I was a pig kicking in the mud. Hours passed, and my stomach rumbled with pain, so I searched for crumbs in corners until I saw a chocolate bar crossing my path. The sound of my teeth chewing made it the most enjoyable meal. It didn't taste like chocolate; it was more like fresh meat with antennae, probably a cockroach, those creatures that seem to survive all kinds of calamities, but at that moment could not escape my hand in search of food.

Being relieved to have written down my dream, I could now focus on preparing for my daughter's birthday party, as she wanted to dress up as a little mermaid.

It was her fifth birthday, and to my surprise, it had already been a year since my mother casually asked me to never take my daughter shopping. When I was four years old (the same age as my daughter at the time), she took me shopping and I was kidnapped for several hours. Devastated, I wasn't prepared to hear such a truth.

Until that moment, I felt like my life was a staircase made of solid bricks, but after hearing her secret, the staircase wobbled and ended up flimsy, made of damp, old cardboard. I couldn't understand how, thirty-one years after the incident, I had never heard anything about it. I asked my mother, and her response was to not ask anyone. But I did the opposite, and asked my older sisters and aunts, but no one said anything. I also went to the police station, but since it had happened so many years ago, there was no record of it. Now, close to my daughter's fifth birthday celebration, my mother decided to tell me everything related to my kidnapping:

"The woman who brought you back home said she'd seen you on a bus. The kidnapper was carrying you when she asked him what kind of relationship was between the two of you because you were white, almost transparent, and his skin was the color of ebony. The kidnapper's answer didn't convince her, so she grabbed you out of his arms and, picking you up, ran off the bus.

Then, you gave her your phone number, she called the house, and I was the only one there when she brought you."

"What do you mean? No one else saw her?"

"Yes, no one else. And stop asking. Nothing happened, you hear me."

"That's all?"

"Yes. Do you want me to go with you to buy the mermaid costume?"

"Of course, you know I don't like to go shopping."

Hurrying, I tied my hair in a long ponytail and grabbed a blue shirt and a pair of jeans I hadn't worn in a while.

That afternoon we crossed the city on a mission to find the little mermaid costume. My daughter, excited by the chiffon dress in blue, pink, red, yellow, and green, like any other little girl, began to play with the dress. Her hands and little head were under the dress when I began to feel a hot river of adrenaline running through my veins. It was as if I had already experienced it, like a premonition. This time, I didn't feel like I was drowning, and my mother and I were ready to hold her tight and protect her from any shark. So, after holding her little hand, we paid for the costume and headed home.

Tuesday arrived, and with my homework done, I showed up for the scheduled appointment, happy to be able to go shopping without the threat of feeling my heart racing and shortness of breath.

After greeting him, like the good private detective he was, he was ready to show me what he had gotten, but I couldn't hold back and told him what I experienced in the store.

"I'm so happy. Last Sunday, my mother and I went shopping for a costume for my daughter, and for the first time, I only felt my heart racing. I didn't choke, and I was able to finish the purchase. I think that deep inside the labyrinths of my memory are healed, or perhaps that episode in my life is dormant."

"Well, I am happy for you. But first, let me show you what I got: You are incredibly lucky that the store where the kidnapping took place still exists, and in their books, it is noted that on June 21, 1970, there was a kidnapping around 10:00 a.m. The girl (in this case, you) was four years old and was dressed in a yellow flowered dress."

"Ah, that explains why I dreamed I was in a meadow picking flowers."

"Your mother, according to what I noted in these observations, was dressed in a navy blue, white-striped, sailor-style suit."

"Ah, in my dream she was wearing jeans, but the fact that she was wearing a navy-blue suit might explain why I was swimming in the clear ocean in my dream."

"What are you talking about?"

"It's Okay. It was a dream I had. Please continue."

"Another of my findings is that it happened on a rainy day, and the roof of the store was leaking near where the kidnapping took place."

"Perhaps that can explain why I was kicking around in the mud in my dream and now I make sculptures. You see, water plus dirt results in clay, and my sculptures are made of clay."

"Ma'am, I don't understand what you are saying. Let me finish."

"Of course, go on."

"Based on police records, an old man was stationed outside the store and described the kidnapper as being around forty years old, dark-skinned, and fat."

"Suddenly, my heart started beating and pointing to a nearby table in a trembling voice, I said, "Like that man in the photo."

"Yes."

"Who is he? His face looks familiar."

"Ma'am, that was me when I was younger."

"Well, just tell me how you know what the kidnapper looked like and how you got the police records. I tried, but the police station told me there was no information."

"Ma'am, I have my contacts. Relax. Do you want to save the rest for another appointment?"

"No. I'm fine. Don't worry about me. I'm listening."

"The police report says the man put you on the bus. The station also received information that he was seen with you near a brick building on Amapola Street and that a large sum of money was paid for your ransom. The woman who took you home was his accomplice."

"Really?"

"Yes, and they both got away with it. Ma'am, everything points to it being a kidnapping for money. At the hospital, the records indicate there was no physical abuse, just some marks on your arms from when the kidnapper took you from your hiding place. Do you want to tell me something about your dream?"

"Well, my mother never wore jeans or had her hair tied back in a ponytail. That's more my style, but the fact that in your notes she appears to be wearing a navy-blue suit makes it more believable."

"Well, you know you can't believe 100 percent in dreams."

"Yes, you may be right. Anyway, in my dream I also saw the apartment where he had me kidnapped."

"So, how do you feel? Is it a closed chapter in your life, or do you still want to find a psychologist to hypnotize you?"

"No, I'm happy with your work. I'm not going to dig any deeper. Thank you very much, and here's what I owe you."

"Give the check to my secretary on the way out. It's been a pleasure working for you."

Grabbing my bag, I tucked my glasses into my hair, left his office, and headed down the stairs just as the detective made a phone call.

"She's gone and she's satisfied," the detective said to someone at the other end of the line. "She also said she's not going to dig any deeper into it. You don't have to worry about anything anymore."

"Good," a woman's voice said. "I hope that episode in her life remains dormant."

"Only time will tell."

"Yes, only time will tell, and no matter what happens, my daughter must never find out about how we tricked her father into paying the ransom."

"Yes, and I still find it hard to believe that you were married to that man."

"At least we stopped him from leaving me

homeless. That's all he wanted, and to think we were so many years together only to abandon me for a 20-year-old."

"My love, stop torturing yourself."

"You're right. See you later."

"Okay," said the old, fat, dark-skinned man, wiping excess sweat from his hands with a handkerchief."

Federica

The arrival of Federica Valdez brought great expectations to the fifth-grade girls at School the Angelinas. A decent girls' school where good manners and the development of moral character and intellect were the guidelines to be followed. Located at the top of the hill, the colonial-style school stands out for its arabesque arches, terracotta floors, and red-tiled roofs. On her first day at school, the teacher welcomed Federica and encouraged the other students to show her the school facilities.

Federica looked like a model out of a postcard; her navy-blue jumper with red plaid contrasted with her long blond hair and blue eyes. The hem of her skirt was just right, falling to the center of her knees where it met her white stockings. Slim as a model, she was made to walk the hallways several times, emphasizing the importance of not exposing any skin. The girls were also not allowed to have long, polished nails, chains, or rings, only the baptismal medal or cross.

Every morning, they had to undergo inspection, and those who violated the rules were sent home. The remaining girls went to the chapel to pray to the rosary and the litanies.

Every day all pupils went to church, and the altar, made of gold leaves, displayed the holy family, as well as cherubs hovering in great splendor.

A week had passed, and Federica still hadn't

spoken to anyone; she only heard the timbre of her voice when she answered the teachers' questions. This wasn't because she was shy, but because no one wanted to be her friend.

The other girls looked at her with suspicion because, as the daughter of diplomats, they knew she had lived in various places and spoke strange words, making her the favorite student in English and French classes.

For the first time, Graciela, the most popular girl in the class, along with Carolina and Patricia, took her to the cafeteria to try the typical Venezuelan lunch (shredded beef patties with passion fruit juice). Satisfied, before the recess ended, they quickly went to the park.

The silence reigned in the cafeteria; her classmates didn't say a word, but Federica hoped that they would play with her on the seesaw, the wheel, or the swings to make it an unforgettable afternoon.

Confused, Federica wondered why they went straight ahead, without first playing on the seesaw, the wheel, and the swings.

"Where are we going?" asked Federica.

"Walk," said Graciela, pointing with her arm outstretched at the Araguaney tree looming in the distance.

"Why are we going all the way there? We have to walk a long way."

"Walk, Federica, you'll like it."

Quickly, Carolina and Patricia held Federica against the trunk of the leafy Araguaney tree, dotted with yellow flowers, while Graciela forced her mouth open with her hands, stuffing it with flowers.

"That's how you'll be! Quiet, quiet, quiet! We

don't want to hear your voice or your strange words anymore. Here at this school, you won't have any friends, and you'll have to be invisible. We don't want you around, do you understand?"

Federica's eyes were about to burst into tears when Graciela said:

"And if you're going to cry, you'd better say you fell. The bells are already ringing, it's time to go to class. Hurry up, and you, Federica, don't walk with us. We don't want others to think we are your friends."

Spitting out the petals and yellow flowers one by one, Federica adjusted her jumper and walked alone to the classroom.

Months pass of being alone in the cafeteria and at recess, with only the doll on duty for company. Dolls that came with their own suitcase and closet to store unused clothes and shoes.

Every day Federica arrived with a different doll, and there were no longer forty or fifty different dolls; she was on number one hundred, and there were still months left until the end of the school year.

The girls' curiosity began to manifest, and rumors circulated that she owned three hundred dolls and that the entire second floor of her house was her playroom. Through casual conversations, they learned that her birthday party would soon be held. After refreshments, a magician's performance, and clowns, Federica would give away dolls specially brought from Spain at the end of the party. She hadn't yet decided who to invite. It would only be those who were kind to her.

Graciela, Carolina, and Patricia, being the most popular, couldn't be left out of such an event, so they tried to gain back her trust.

The afternoon Federica showed up with "Mariquita Perez," dressed in her Valencian brocade dress, she needed help with her hair. As the dress required, she had to make two long braids, twist them into a lock next to each ear, and place the golden combs on each side. Also, in the center of her head, she would wear the largest comb.

Pearl accessories, such as earrings and hairpins of different sizes, would add the finishing touch of elegance.

Pretending to be a hairdresser, Federica asked for help, and in moments, Graciela, Carolina, and Patricia were under her command and played with her all afternoon.

The next morning, the three of them were ready to follow Federica's orders. Like automatons, they sat in a circle with the book in the center. Federica began the ritual:

"Graciela, Carolina, and Patricia, raise your hands to the sky and repeat: Forces of good and evil, through this book, with the help of the wind, show us the truth."

Federica took the thick book and placed it face up, between the pages, in the middle of it, stuck the scissors in the center. Then she took the black ribbon, placed it under the flap, stretched the ends of the ribbon upward, twisting each ribbon through the blades of the scissors, while tying three knots.

"Patricia: Place your index finger in the eyelet of the scissors. You, Carolina, do the same. Now, close your eyes. And I'll ask the questions:"

"Who will bring my books? And the book leaned toward Graciela.

"Who will bring the doll?" she asked. And the book leaned toward Carolina.

"Who will give me weekly money? she asked. And the book leaned toward Patricia.

For a whole week, Graciela would bring her books, Carolina would carry the chosen doll, and Patricia would give her money to buy whatever lunch she wanted.

Every week, Federica took some girl's money, and every day, she received favors from her classmates, even though she treated them with disdain.

Federica was now the most popular girl in the class, and every day there were more rumors about her future party.

The day of the party was approaching, and Federica still hadn't said who she would invite. She just continued to enjoy the favors of others, just as she enjoyed the pranks she invented.

That afternoon, after Federica tripped her, Graciela was taken to the infirmary. As she fell, she scraped her face and elbows. Graciela, after Federica's withering look, immediately stopped crying. She knew she should not blame her, as the possibility of being invited to her birthday party was getting closer every day.

Holy Week arrived, and at daily Mass they noticed Federica's absence. Was she sick? Who knows? But it had been several days since they'd seen her.

All the teachers did was whisper, until the girls, seeing how close the birthday was, began to ask: "is Federica sick? is she having her own party? who is she going to invite?"

"What? No one has told you. Federica and her parents have left! Her father has been transferred, and it won't be a party. However, she has left a basket full of packages that will be delivered on Palm Sunday," said the teacher.

The Palm Sunday Mass ended. The palm crosses were handed out, and on the way out each girl took a package from the basket.

Gathered outside the chapel, an order was given to everyone to open their gifts.

Clicks were heard as small hands manipulated the cellophane paper, and suddenly the face, the smile of the doll specially brought from Spain that resembles Federica. Boxed dolls, whose faces mirrored Federica's.

All the girls burst into tears and threw the dolls away, a reminder of so much redress.

"Don't cry, girls, there was no party, but there was a doll..."

The Raven

"You were born alone, and you will die alone," was the wise advice she should follow to achieve something of her own and not, in return, be an appendage of Ernesto. In a society where women were expected to be exclusively servants to serve their husbands and please them in every way, in a society where women didn't have the right to vote, where their place of dominion was limited to the home and the management of the servants, (although, behind every big deal, feminine subtlety always delivered the final blow,) mom Antonia, ahead of her time, broke with all conventions, the hotel, located on the dead end of Candil street, was entirely managed by her, so her life was spent among travelers looking for a long or short stay. Since she was never married, from a young age she demanded that I not give her that displeasure...

Getting married would be like burying myself alive, she told me, and being buried alive was what Ernesto feared most. With frequent bouts of claustrophobia, he couldn't stay in a closed space for more than a few minutes. His labored breathing and cold sweats were the most noticeable signs of the anguish he suffered. His claustrophobia, which turned into paranoia, was so strong that the mere thought of being controlled by someone suffocated him, and it was clear he would never sign the marriage contract. Mama Antonia loved Ernesto for me, because she didn't see in him the threat of holding me down. Ours was a relationship that scandalized the entire town, except for her.

My union with Ernesto was fresh and spontaneous. He came to visit me in the afternoons, and without a chaperone, we would leave through the back of the field planted with mango and avocado trees. Our conversations revolved around what was happening in the town and his plans as a future doctor, since in a few months he would graduate and be able to practice psychiatry at the asylum on the hill.

Ernesto spent long hours of the day among books and papers. He read incessantly. He wasn't afraid of interruptions, as he had no known family or friendship ties. He only had daily conversations with me, and I still knew nothing of his past. Reserved as he was, his dream was to penetrate the world of the "forgotten" in the asylum "The Raven", a house in the purest Spanish style, which had been occupied during the conquest by the unfortunate Spanish soldiers who were imprisoned there. In the twentieth century, it still retained wrought iron gates and cells so incredibly small that a man of that time could barely lie with his limbs touching the walls. It was so named, "The Raven," because it was built with black rocks, and because it symbolized death itself, surrounded by hungry crows who, during the night, devoured the food scraps left in the garbage bags at the end of the day.

Ernesto's graduation was successful. The town's leading doctor took him on as a pupil. Many doors began to open in his professional career, among them, the tempting opportunity to move to the capital after completing his internship at the asylum. Eager to end our relationship, he began to change: his vulgar comments, coupled with psychological and physical abuse, contributed to undermining me psychologically. The unbearable situation led me to being admitted to "The Raven" for two months for a sleep cure.

A week prior to the admittance, I tried to acclimatize myself to the routine of the asylum. I knew I would be asleep, but I wanted to experience my surroundings. The afternoon promised a beautiful walk through the gardens, when, sitting on a bench, I tried to converse with Irene, a patient who, at the approach of any doctor, began to scream, visibly upset by the cocktails of pills she was given daily. The poor woman had already been in the institution for three years. Curious to know more about her, I tried to dig into the archives: she had been confined for apparent insanity. Surprised, I read that she had been admitted by her own husband, the now Dr. Ernesto, my Ernesto, who had been her husband for five years. And he had led me to believe he had never been married.

The day scheduled for my sleep cure was approaching. I feared Ernesto's presence the night of March 13th when I saw him, syringe in hand, trying to put me to sleep. He knew I shared his secret, and, refusing to accept any past that bound him, or anyone who knew the facts of his life, he had decided to silence me forever. The papers indicated it was a doctor's order to inject me. Knowing that my screams would be of no use, I resisted being injected. Terrified, I refused to let myself be pricked, staring at the syringe with the lethal liquid that, thanks to Irene's unexpected help and the three of us struggling with a miraculous twist of fate, ended up in Ernesto's veins.

The Dance of the Shadows

Ernesto, terrified by the horror of confinement, the cold sweats, and tachycardia, stared blankly, unable to even blink. The doctors, perplexed by the unexpected situation, contemplated Ernesto as in a comma, his vital signs diminished, declared themselves unable to return him to normal, while I searched for Irene to help her get out and free her from the imposing black crow, which, in precise flights, was looking for fresh meat to devour.

Maria Gabriela Madrid

Goal!

Goal! The World Cup, eagerly awaited every four years, is intended to ease the routine of the average fan. This time, viewers have a better schedule, from morning until three in the afternoon, and broadcast again at night. Unlike four years ago, when the games were broadcast in the early hours. This redress didn't prevent twenty-two million people from enjoying such a colorful spectacle. Now, spectators, pretending to extend their lunch break, skip work with excuses, feigning illness. Others, without a television within reach, lock themselves in the bathrooms to listen to the radio broadcast.

Goal!... Germany bursting with joy and disappointment. Fans waving their national flag high. Fans equipped with party favors, garlands, bugles, and drums. Young teams make unexpected moves. Veteran teams seek to stay in power. There's Gisela, watching television, that empty box, hoping her heart will race with another Goal! Empty beer bottles. On the grill, with the blueish coals, the blood sausages, potatoes, and chopped onions are roasting, allowing the aromas to spread, mingling with the aroma of raw meat. The blood sausage is the most desired, even though it's just coagulated blood awaiting the lucky fang. No one thinks about mad cow disease. Everyone, like in Russian roulette, hopes not to win. And goal, the chosen team is winning, and goal, they just tied... And goal, we are losing...

Blurred, tense, and sad faces witness the few seconds left until the game ends. Men going through a midlife crisis seek solitude, a chance to enjoy the games without the presence of their children's mothers, weary women awaiting the result. Rogelio knows this won't be an ordinary match. It will be a fight to the death, and just thinking about it makes the blood sausage, and meat churn in his stomach, causing uncontrollable heartburn and nausea that makes him vomit, spilling vomit into the living room and staining the sofa. Ashamed, he asks Gisela to get the sponge to clean it up. The disgusting odor forces those present to go outside.

The fans have formed two teams: husbands versus wives, four against three, as Isabela died last year. The beautiful landscape of the Grand Canyon had been a silent witness to the tragic accident: Isabela dangling, swinging, screaming, and crying until the rope snapped. Everyone waits for Gisela to arrive to start the match. Adrenaline is at its highest level. They coordinate their moves and run in search of a goal, while also calculating how to avoid the cars passing on the road. Rogelio, dismissed from the game for tripping someone, went to buy some medicine. While Gisela continued playing, eager to score, she didn't notice the car approaching and was hit by Rogelio, who was driving back with Pepto-Bismol. Red card, out of the game, he watched as his wife's lifeless body lay in the ditch, her beautiful face, with its black hair, rolled and rolled and rolled in slow motion until he scored the goal.

Unfazed, the witnesses of the sinister spectacle didn't know what to do, didn't know how to react to the head that stopped in the net, that lifeless face that gave them the victory cup. Four men and two women witnessed how blood, sweat, and tears yielded the final score. Couples engaged in extreme sports. They, the wives, try to share their time. They, the husbands, seek to escape.

Fran and Rogelio, now free, regress fifteen years. The other two will continue to devise ways to escape one day.

Insane Abandonment

That morning, undoubtedly different from others, the daily goodbye kiss felt empty and distant. I noticed his lost gaze, feeling as if it pierced me, contrary to our usual farewell. It had been months of mystery in which I couldn't guess what my husband was thinking. Was it a problem at work? Another woman, perhaps? Today I realized what Aunt Ines always told me about Uncle Jorge, who went out one afternoon to buy the newspaper, never to return.

When Rodolfo said goodbye that morning, I had the feeling he would not be returning.

After her husband disappeared, Aunt Ines began an arduous search, fruitless, and even came to believe he was just another of the missing. Without taking a break, she shouted with a banner in the Plaza de Mayo. Uncle Jorge had participated in the dissident movement, distributing revolutionary leaflets, and they might have caught him. This thought was more tolerable for someone who, terrified, had taken advantage of their current situation to escape the tedious routine of a marriage that had already lasted twenty years, leaving only the memories of a life together, full of joys and disappointments.

What had happened to Rodolfo? I wondered. Will he come back? My head was almost exploding just imagining that he had abandoned me. Like a hammer pounding blows in my brain, the pain increased.

Desperate, I resorted to the unexpected: I wouldn't allow Rodolfo, the love of my youth, to leave me alone in this overcrowded world, without the necessary resources to survive. In my agony, faced with the decision I had made, I opted to make myself a drink, a screwdriver, our favorite drink. But this time I would add phenobarbital pills, the ones he took daily. The effect of the drug, combined with the alcohol, ensured I would sleep peacefully to never wake up.

The glass of orange juice with gin and crushed ice, plus the pills, was already ready. Ready to take it, I felt the overwhelming urge to vomit. My nerves had attacked not only my brain, but also my stomach, which was twisting at the imminence of certain death. Running, I went to the bathroom and stayed in until Rodolfo returned.

Tired from a day of work and having remembered our anniversary for the first time, Rodolfo was debating what gift to bring me: it would be red and orange flowers, like the orange color of the "drink" I'd prepared and left on the living room table. Exhausted, he untied his tie and, trying to relax, downed the drink, while I, unaware of his arrival, remained locked in the bathroom, trying not to faint. Suddenly, a loud bang broke the silence that surrounded me. Distraught, I went to the living room, and there he was, collapsed on the carpet. From his half-open mouth flowed a blackish liquid, perhaps from the futile effort to vomit. His lifeless face, white and pale, showed the anguish of the incomprehensible. A single gulp and the desire to rest had been enough. Now he was dead and alone. I hugged my husband's corpse, certain

The Dance of the Shadows

that he would never abandon me, although always, from beyond the grave, he would ask me: "Why?"

Socks

On any given Sunday, the laundry lay waiting to be sorted and washed. There were knotted socks, ready to drown in the warm and cold-water cycles. While other socks, alone, would search inside the washing machine for their soulmate. The single ones, left-handed or right-handed, would be the unfortunate ones who wouldn't feel the warmth of the dryer's warm air.

The overflowing laundry basket begged to be emptied. There was no room left for any shirts, pants, panties, or socks, but Roco (the sock) needed to know what had happened to his Rosita. Wriggling, he slid down, began to climb the wicker basket, and finally, panting, managed to climb over the edge. Roco knew that now he would be entering the washing machine, so, anticipating the long-fingered hand, he made Mustard spit him out from the breakfast nook for the last time. It would no longer be due to the uncontrollable passion that once united them, but rather to Roco's pleas for help getting him back to Rosita. Roco knew that being dirty would help him avoid confusion with the almost clean ones, and the search would be faster. Rosita, aware of his recent chance encounters with Mustard, would recognize the disgusting smell and be able to identify Roco from any distance.

Everyone huddled together, anticipating the first round, the first cycle of hot water and soap. Roco felt fearful because he had never been washed before, but his passion for knowing about Rosita minimized any anxiety. Wet with the white foam, Roco mingled unnoticed with the rest of the laundry. Searching and searching, he turned and turned, until he spotted Rosita's pink tip in the distance.

I'll catch up with you in another turn, he repeated to himself.

And the turns came, one, two, three, and four, and Rosita was still far away, when suddenly, the clothes next to Roco began to separate.

The smell of rotten mustard hadn't been removed with the usual soap. Only a chlorine-based soap could give it the proper fragrance. Now with the path clear, and with a few twists and turns, he caught up with Rosita, and she, driven away by the bad smell, rolled around and fled from him.

"Wait, Rosita, wait! Understand that it's you I want. Let us tie ourselves together so we don't lose each other and can enjoy the warmth that awaits us."

"I can't, Roco, I can't. I loved you too, or maybe I still do, but I just cannot stand that smell you are carrying. For us to talk, you will have to wait for them to wash you with bleach."

"Who knows if they will do it, Rosita Please give me another chance."

Suddenly, the long-fingered hand appeared and, taking the freshly washed clothes, put them in the dryer, leaving Roco alone in the corner with the mustard on it.

Rosita, without a companion, ended up in the dryer, but between each turn, the air helped to knot her around a solitary sock, allowing them, engulfed by the fragrant fragrance, to merge into one. A knot in stockings

where the one with the long-fingered hand will never
know the passion that consumed them.

That Unforgettable Day

Saturday, April 13th. Six in the morning. Francisco, in a hurry, looks for the locks for his suitcases. Before traveling, he wants to avoid the risk of having his belongings stolen or being accused of carrying illegal items. Disturbed, he lifts the cushions, throwing his clothes on the floor in search of locks. As soon as he finds them, he runs to the bathroom to look at himself in the mirror. Fifteen minutes of combing his hair to fix the four remaining hairs, simulating the look of the 1930s: slicked back, shiny, keeping away anyone who might try to touch it.

Hearing the horn of the taxi, he waits impatiently for the elevator to arrive. Once in the taxi, he asks the driver to speed up, and they finally arrive at the airport. The flight is delayed. He must wait an hour before boarding. The purpose of the trip is to visit his girlfriend after three months of separation. The engagement ring, a diamond solitaire bought with his first paycheck, bulges out of the side pocket of his jacket.

Francisco has just finished a master's degree in tourism. The internship at the Waldorf-Astoria was fruitful; he learned how the hotel works and participated in all the departments, liking the least the laundry department, where he changed the sheets on the twelfth floor for three consecutive weeks. Now he feels ready to have his own hotel. It will be small, an easy-to-manage bed and breakfast. He will talk to Irene about it, as they already must look for a location. Francisco daydreams: once married, they will move to New York City to try their luck...

The plane took off. The flight was smooth until it began to shake. Constant turbulence and a feeling of emptiness made him vomit. Grateful for arriving safely, and appreciative of the pilot's efforts, he subsequently discovered that his suitcases had been slashed. New, expensive suitcases made of fine fabric ripped, by criminals who stole the suits, sweaters, bow ties, and patent leather shoes. Having filled out the claim form, he can only hope that one day he will receive money in return.

The car he rented was not the one he wanted; the one he had reserved was crashed by the driver who was supposed to deliver it. Now he drives an ivory Fiat. He will make the trip to Irene's house as soon as possible; he wants to see her, hold her, caress her, kiss her, and without further ado, gives her the ring he'd worked so hard to buy. At the curve in the road, at the intersection of Interstate 70, a tire burst. He stoically changed it, unable to believe what had happened, and, tightening the last screw, drops of rain and gusts of wind blackened the sky, unleashing a storm that forced him to slow down. What had happened was already a sign that he should have interrupted their plans, but Francisco, a practical man, doesn't believe anything he can't prove. He knows Irene is in the house because she must have already returned from work, and what better way to receive a surprise visit from his beloved.

The Victorian-style house has four bedrooms and two bathrooms. Classical music emanates from the dimly lit living room. To surprise her, he decided to turn around and enter through the back sliding door. Large vases decorate the side tables, and on the center table, two naked bodies squirm between kisses and bites, loving each other with great passion. Terrified, Francisco only manages to utter one word: "Bitch!" Dizzy and sweating cold, he collapses onto the sofa. It was at that moment that they noticed his presence. The universe's strong warnings had already told him not to travel, leaving him with only the memory of a day that would have been unforgettable.

Hot Coffee

On the morning of December 12, I woke up feeling uneasy. Truly strange. But not for my mother, who usually said I was a detached person and that I never felt the pain of others as my own. As anyone would say, that day the routine was the same as the day I started working at the coffee place. Every day I took the newspaper out of the plastic bag and placed it on the wooden table near the main window. Marc, the owner of the coffee place, was surprised to see how people walked past the table without reading or even looking at the newspaper. I always told him that newspapers were a thing of the past and the proof was that customers came with their arsenal of technology like I-pods, iPads, iPhones, computers, and more... But he always insisted on giving the newspaper another chance, so for another day, the newspaper sat on the table, waiting for anyone who wanted to turn the pages and read it.

As I approached the register, a woman in her thirties asked, "What kind of coffee do you sell?"

"I have a macchiato, a cappuccino, a latte..."

"Just give me regular coffee," said the woman with a grimace of annoyance, as if she was losing patience.

"What size do you want? Tall or Large?"

"Small."

"I guess you mean Tall."

"Yes, Tall."

"Is that all, or would you like to buy the newspaper?"

"Just give me the coffee. I read the news online. Besides, who reads newspapers?"

"Well, only those who want to see the pictures. It seems newspapers are a thing of the past for you."

"Yes, you're right."

Turning around, the woman grabbed her coffee and began working on her computer while listening to music on her iPod.

Marc sat down to read the newspaper while he waited for his morning coffee. Suddenly, as I approached his table, I noticed a look of terror on his face, and he instantly jumped up from his chair and grabbed my arm, forcing me to look at a photo of me taken twenty years ago. Even though the photo had poor resolution, it was on the front page of the newspaper so people could learn about my criminal past. Defending myself as best I could from his unexpected act of violence, I threw the hot coffee cup in his face and grabbed the coffee pot, knocking him out and leaving him unconscious on the floor. When I turned around, I noticed the woman still unaware of what was happening around her, she was continuing typing on her computer and listening to music on her iPod. I quickly closed the door, flipped the sign (Open to Closed), drew the curtains, and grabbed the sharpest knife available to slash the woman's neck. The river of blood that flowed from the aorta brought back memories of when I had also killed my parents and siblings with a knife. They wanted to call the police to send me away, to a mental asylum. The way they looked at me at that time was the same way Marc looked at me.

That is how I knew he, too, wanted to call the police to send me away. Quickly, I cut the bodies into small pieces and stuffed them into backpacks. Now, thinking about what happened, maybe my mom was right when she said I have a personality that's indifferent to the pain of others. Who knows?

After hours had passed, and after carefully cleaning up the crime scene, I had a cup of black coffee and walked away to start a new life, perhaps as an employee at a nearby coffee place.

Longing to Breathe

Being at Marion's house was a paradise for my senses: her house, filled with art objects, displays of contemporary and realistic paintings, ethnic sculptures, and colorful walls that reflect the colors of the rainbow. Every time I entered the kitchen, I remembered the collection of different plates, pots, and crockery with floral designs ready to host the day's dishes. The kitchen, like the heart of the house, vibrates with sweet and savory spices waiting to be used. Marion always takes the time to describe everything, and automatically, in the alleys of my mind, endless images recreate what I saw before I lost sight.

As soon as she heard the tap of my white cane approaching, she took the cookies out of the oven and placed them on the plate to cool. The smell that floated in the air was powerful, sweet, and mysterious, because when cooking, she always used a variety of spices that made it difficult for me to determine their place of origin.

"Liz, welcome back! Keep walking straight. It's wonderful that you're here."

"Marion, I'm happy to be here."

"How was your trip? You must tell me everything."

"Marion, it was more than a trip. It was the most enriching experience I could have had. I brought a powder that will take you through the most glorious, deepest, and darkest parts of your soul. It will bring up your past and recent memories. By using it, you will have a better understanding of the good and bad in your spirit. The only rule is to add the powder to your recipe and eat your creation. The only caveat is that each side of your spirit can take over the other and change your soul for better or worse."

"Do you think so?"

"Well, that's what they told me. Why don't we make the cookies for the contest with the Haitian powder?"

"Fine but first let me bring the ingredients to the table."

Feeling anxious about not knowing what to expect, Marion and I put our hands into action. The contact of our cold fingers with the flour made us creative and playful. Then, after mixing the flour with butter, milk, sugar, and salt, we made small balls. The first one was shapeless, but the last was completely round, waiting to be flattened and placed in the oven.

"Wait," Marion said. "You have to add more spices and a little of that powder. Do you still want to add some of that powder you brought from Haiti?"

"Yes, trust me."

"Okay, Liz, here it is. Just move your hand forward a little so you can touch it."

With her eyes closed, Liz took a pinch of spices, and the powder brought from Haiti. Without expecting it, she suddenly felt her heart pound as she remembered the bright colors, the simple and intricate shapes of nature, and the people she had been friends with before the accident, and now they were just part of her memories. The expression on her face ran through all the emotions:

happiness, pleasure, incomprehension, and melancholy. Taking a towel, she removed the excess flour from her hands and with a simple gesture, removed the saltwater running down her cheeks.

"Marion, it does work. I barely touched it and…"

"Come on, Liz," Marion said. "We don't have much time. Place them in the oven."

The heat from the oven quickly baked the cookies, and as soon as they were ready, Liz took them out of the oven, ate one of them, and put the rest on the baking sheet. The strong, sweet smell of cinnamon made Marion salivate. Just as Marion was about to taste the cookie, the phone rang several times. Marion, putting the cookie aside, picked up the receiver instead.

"Liz it was Julia over the phone. She wants to come and try our recipe."

"But Marion, we can't trust her. She's a hypocrite, and you never know what she's thinking. She might come and steal our recipe. Marion, listen to me, she's a tiger in sheep's clothing, and I'm sure she only wants to hurt us."

"No, I think you're exaggerating. She's not coming to steal from us. You know her; she's your sister, and maybe she just wants to make peace with you."

"Stop talking, she's here. I can feel her presence, and she's about to ring the doorbell."

Julia walked slowly, folding her skirt to keep her cookies from getting wet in the rain.

"Howdy, here are the cookies that will win the contest."

"Okay, Julia, ours will be hard to beat. Don't count on winning."

"Liz don't be mean to me. I had nothing to do with your accident. It's not my fault I wasn't there for you."

"Well, it's actually very convenient for you, because that way you've ended up being the sole heir to our parents' fortune, and now you even have a say in my future."

"Liz, I swear that if you behave yourself, doing what I say, I'll never send you to any institution and I'll even let you live with me in the house. Come on, let's make up."

Furious at what her sister had said, Liz went to the kitchen cupboard. Not long ago, she had won most of the horse ridings competitions in South Texas. Her riding style and maneuvers distinguished her from the rest of the competitors. She had not only become a legend but was a free spirit, now trapped in the darkness and at the mercy of her sister's decisions.

Desperate, Liz felt every can and package of food until she almost fell over a bag of rat poison.

"Liz, do you need any help? The cookies are ready."

"I'm fine. Just wait, I will sprinkle them with sugar. I'll be right there."

Approaching the table, Liz said, "the cookies are sprinkled and are ready."

"Liz, are you better? No more fighting?"

"Of course. Don't think about it. I'm fine. Marion, I already sprinkled mine. Just sprinkle some more on Julia's and yours."

With a swift movement, Marion sprinkled both of their cookies several times.

After eating them, Julia watched as Marion's

rocking chair stopped moving and her hand suddenly fell to the side as she knocked the rest of the cookie onto the floor.

Distraught and terrified, Julia tried to revive Marion. Her lifeless body left her with the unavoidable truth that she would be next. Desperate, she made futile attempts to vomit up the poisoned cookies.

"Liz, look what you've done."

"Little sister not to worry. You don't have much time left, so to speak. Marion is waiting for you. And as for me, everyone will think it was an accident. I'm just a blind woman who gave the two of you rat poison instead of sugar. I told you, Julia, that I'd always have my freedom. Now I'll be the sole heir to our parents' fortune, and no one listen carefully is going to decide my life. Go on, finish dying. You only have a few more minutes to live."

Meanwhile, Liz, with a triumphant look, picked up the receiver and called the police at the same time Julia, anxious, expired the last breath.

Maria Gabriela Madrid

Black and White

Priest Pablo is losing strength. The battle has been long for the inhabitants of that town, divided between followers of the Ifa oracle and those of the Catholic religion. Although Catholicism displays a religious syncretism with the feast of Saint Benedict, celebrated to the rhythm of drums, colorful costumes, and rum, Father Pablo was unwilling to mediate with the followers of Ifa, descendants of the Yoruba, who arrived with songs and rituals to the region where, since ancient times, they had practiced animal sacrifice with the intention of warding off evils and transferring human illnesses to the sacrificed animal, thus freeing the spirit of the affected person from negative forces.

The church, with its ever-declining attendance, faces the square (presided over by a statue of Simon Bolivar riding for freedom), surrounded by cobblestone streets that denote the three hundred years that have passed since the founding of that industrial town, where oil wells and the trade of basic goods constitute the mainstay of its economy.

The population, made up of indigenous people, suffers from a growing illiteracy rate. Some converts saw in Father Pablo's oratory a link to the outside world as well as a window to heaven that would give them spiritual peace and encouragement to continue with their daily work. Everything was routine, until one Sunday, Father Pablo, with a fiery speech, shook the entire town, including those who had not attended Sunday Mass and learned, through secondhand sources, of what had happened that morning.

Deeply distressed by the division marked by religious differences, the priest woke up fearfully and decided that only he, as a soldier of Christ, could demand unconditional support from the faithful. To change the situation, he decided to tell them about the dream he had the night before. The atmosphere in the church was dense and humid, the silence was total, and only the priest's rapid breathing could be heard as he recounted how he had seen the square, the church, and the cobblestone streets stained with blood, corpses scattered everywhere, and the wails of souls in torment carried by the dawn wind. He interpreted this as a sign that the year 2000 was approaching and, as the apocalypse indicated, Satan would be unleashed. He predicted that the battle between good and evil was approaching. Those who practiced any activity other than that of increasing the Christian faith must be persecuted. Among these practices was "Santeria", and any other irrational activity that violated faith in the creator God. Staring at them, he shouted at those who witnessed the church's stained-glass windows ringing: "the beast may already be among us, or he may be about to arrive. Look for the signs, for later Our Lord will reward you."

That day, the priest formed a committee. Filomena Buenano would receive and review newcomers; the priest would hear confessions daily; the judicial system would pursue enemies and those marked as Satan's followers.

Everyone was prepared to catch the devil. They

knew he could take any disguise, any form of representation, from a newborn to the most vulnerable elderly, even any animal figure, always with the purpose of camouflaging himself among the people and going unnoticed. Panic had broken out, and fear was evident in the inhabitants' expressions, and they could no longer trust even their own families. In the following three years, numerous people were burned in the moonlight simply for exhibiting strange behavior or habits that distanced them from God.

The descendants of slaves, due to their customs, were the most persecuted. The chants in foreign languages and the custom of sacrificing animals, always surrounded by lit candles, indicated that they were followers of evil. The purges continued, and the person in charge of such arduous work, Filomena Buenano, whose corpulent physique protected her soul from the snares of evil, continued to be the most admired by the townspeople. At every birth she attended, she constantly scrutinized the newborn, always looking for the "three sixes" or the "pentagon within the circle," unmistakable signs of the devil.

One night, feeling unwell, Filomena sent Teresa, her assistant, to Dolores's house. Dolores was already the mother of four children and about to give birth to her fifth. Dolores was complaining. The tearing of her skin announced the imminent arrival of the long-awaited baby, while a violent storm shook the foundations of the stilt house. Water ran through the old wood and blood gushed from Dolores's body until a pale, swaddled baby girl was born.

After a few moments, the storm ceased, as if it

had served as a backdrop for the event.

The newborn's name would be biblical: Ana Gabriel, from a young age, she would learn to survive by collecting cans to exchange money to buy the day's food. One afternoon, while walking along the lakeshore, she found herself floating in the air due to a huge explosion. Oil well number G3-5 had collapsed. The waters covered her entire body, now filled with black gold leeches. She was carried on shoulders to the hospital, and hours later, she woke up alone. She left the hospital on the sixth day of the sixth month of 1996, while a tense calm reigned in the town and everyone whispered about what had happened to Ana Gabriel.

Eager to look for signs of the beast, everyone looked at the young girl with suspicion. Her unexpected muteness forced her to write, but the letters came out backward. Mirror-like writing. No one wanted to see her, but she wrote: "When the "Black gold" runs out it will leave everyone in darkness."

"Witch, witch, witch they shouted incessantly."

Was she perhaps the devil's helper? Or perhaps the devil himself disguised himself to create fear in the region? Just imagining that they might run out of their black gold, sent by God, that if it ran out, it would be times of scarce money, no more commerce, no more electricity. The guardians of the treasure surrounded her, tied her to some logs, and covered her with scraps of newspaper. And they called out to Father Pablo amid chants and prayers, so that the premonitions wouldn't come true and, to prevent him from transforming into a new being at all costs, they lit the scraps of Ana Gabriel' newspaper. Illuminated by the fire, Father Pablo saw in an instant that those around him were witnesses to how his burning eyes rolled back, and he convulsed incessantly in an epileptic fit.

Jose, a resident of the town, remembering that the priest had mentioned in one of his sermons that epilepsy was a manifestation of Satan, alerted those present, who, shuddering, picked him up on their shoulders and, without much thought, threw him with great force into the bonfire. Amidst the flames and screams of the spectators, their skin charred, mingling with a pile of bones and burnt flesh, until the fire slowly went out. Ana Gabriel no longer looked white and swaddled, as she had at birth. Now she was dark, like the black gold they saw as a gift from God; while at her side, the corpse of Father Pablo, believed by many to be possessed by the devil, mixed with the young woman, next to the coals in a pile of bones and ashes.

Between the Furrows of Memory

Ana Lucia! ANA LUCIA! She heard them but didn't want to see them. On that somber night, she traversed cobblestone streets. The inhabitants of the surrounding estates, lit only by warm oil lamps comparable only to their body temperature, didn't notice her presence. Tired and seeking refuge, she longed to remember the nights of family gatherings that passed without a single worry. Now, everything was so different. Longing for a good plate of food, she remembered the daily meals, with five different dishes placed on the embroidered linen tablecloth. The oak table and the Bohemian crystal glasses, so carefully guarded by Aunt Luisa.

Aunt Luisa, dad's sister, would come down at night to check that everything was in order. In perpetual misery, never met her soul mate, she didn't talk to anyone, and her increasingly frequent night screams shattered the stillness of the night. Meanwhile, Mom Ines, eager for knowledge, devoured every book she could get her hands on. Every three months, a laborer would go to the city with errands, and with luck, he would sometimes acquire a few books. Despite never having traveled, Mom Ines read in several languages. Her perseverance and dedication transported her to the most remote places, experiencing torrid romances. Dad Ramon, her youthful love, was rarely home; trips to the coffee plantations were frequent, and the sordid recollection of the dark furrows, where he had strayed more than once, returned to her memory, stimulated by the fresh aroma of coffee. Catalina and Maria played around, competing to see who would receive the most attention from the servants: the sheets, which at the girls' request were extra warmed up because the hot milk taken before bedtime didn't have the desired effect of warming them.

Catalina was sent to look for a "tente alla", the famous imaginary pill to keep the kids away, and restored peace to those present, and peace was what Ana Lucia desired. Despite the darkness, when only the owls could be heard courting the moon, Ana Lucia ran across the fields until she knocked on the doorbell of Father Pepe's church, located across from the main square, where on Sundays they gave the needy free lunches, a charity that Ana Lucia was now desperately seeking. Abruptly, the young altar boy silently guided her up the spiral staircase and hid her in the attic, near the bell tower. Father Pepe disliked unexpected visitors; he only admitted the homeless on Sundays and at certain times. Due to his earthly, rather than spiritual spirit, he hated helping the destitute.

At sunrise, the altar boy and Ana Lucía set out for the Santa Rita Convent. The journey would last three days and two nights. They walked along the river, the same one where her nanny had taken her to dip her long black hair in the turbulent waters, and the white foam mingled with the blood of the disappeared: the customers of Lola's bar who were no longer "regulars". In the distance, they saw the high walls, witnesses to so much uncertainty and unrest, where, protected from worldly temptations, the nuns lived, trapped with no way of escape.

In her desperation, Ana Lucia chose the safety of that home, where she wouldn't be walled up alive as had happened to her cousin in "Santa Fe of Bogota": letters never answered and the family's complicity in the face of the tragic reality of an unwanted child who would shame the family by staining the family name forever. A true sacrifice to which she was led unprepared, gagged with a mixture of mud and cement that ended her unborn baby and her seventeen-year-old life. Ana Lucia had heard this story so many times from Aunt Luisa that she decided to avoid the same fate as her cousin, although she couldn't forget Fernando and the chance encounters behind the Araguaney' tree, where they both radiated flashes of happiness from the accumulated passion of years, months, weeks, and days.

Oh! Poor Fernando! Having been caught with his underwear down, asking for forgiveness that was of no use to Dad Ramon, who threw him that dark night into the dark furrows of the coffee plantation, where the dogs, after hours of searching, found him.

Terrified, Ana Lucia crossed the gate with her beautiful and painful memories, which would accompany her until the end of her days.

No more laughter from her sisters Catalina and Maria. No more family gatherings, nor the heartbreaking screams of Aunt Luisa, between dark walls and warm oil lamps, in contrast with the temperature of her body, now cold, although free among the furrows of memory.

Maria Gabriela Madrid

The Madrilera

Located in the hilltop roundabout, just two blocks from the church of the Chinese priest, whom everyone views with suspicion, as they don't understand how he can speak Spanish when he looks Asian, The Madrilera was cursed. When Perla Elena went to live in The Madrilera, she had already been informed by the townspeople that only the laborers had been inside, and they told anecdotes about the presence of a moaning spirit. The mansion has five rooms, a kitchen through which the icy channel water comes directly from the river flows, and a bathroom, which at the time it was installed, was considered modern, as it was inside the house, compared to the bathrooms on the neighboring estates, which were merely latrines in the courtyards.

The "crazy woman's room" as it was called in the town remained locked. Grandma Cecilia died there 50 years ago, of typhoid fever, covered with embroidered linen sheets. Fever, sweating, and uncontrollable diarrhea indicated that death was approaching, and at one in the morning, she died. The wake was held in the dining room. On the table, placed against the wall, lit candlesticks were displayed, dimly illuminating the room. Missals and rosaries were also on display, awaiting the mourners to pray for her soul. The widower, General Matias de la Cuesta, driven mad by Cecilia's absence, did not go out again. The servants did all grocery shopping. The gold coins, kept in the trunks, were exchanged for national currency to ensure dignified old age and support for Eduardo, the grandson.

The years passed, and the number of employees grew smaller. The gold coins were no longer enough, and they were managed by young Eduardo, barely eighteen years old, who had to walk four kilometers each way to attend high school. The brown horse had been his father's last gift. Seeing him died suddenly caused him immense sadness. Heartbroken at losing not only his father but also a faithful friend, Eduardo was left alone with the memories of those rides, breaking up the cracked earth of the roads.

One afternoon, Eduardo returned tired, with sores that Perla Elena soothed with cool water. They no longer saw each other as cousins or playmates. The attraction was undeniable, despite the dreaded separation, which was growing ever closer. Late that afternoon, Uncle Juan arrived from the city and advised him to study engineering, therefore once he finished high school, he moved to the capital. In love with Perla Elena, he promised to continue their courtship, sending her letters and visiting her every summer.

The university accepted him, and without wasting any time, he completed his studies until he graduated with honors as an engineer. Building bridges and roads was what he was most passionate about, not building small houses like his colleagues. Meanwhile, his love affair with his cousin, always missing her, winning her over with letters and gifts, lasted for five years, until Perla Elena, in love, brave, adventurous, cultured, and elegant, moved to the big city, where they married. Through financial ups and downs and other vicissitudes, which they always managed to overcome, they raised four children. But the most rewarding thing of all was growing old together, intermittently sharing the children and grandchildren who had provided them with so much love and companionship.

Children, grandchildren, and great-grandchildren visit The Madrilera with trunks full of memories. A mansion inhabited by ghosts, whose intermittent laughter continues to echo in the walls, wandering around in the middle of the night, descending the stairs at three o clock in the morning, leaving crumbs in the kitchen and icy gusts, no longer so gloomy, for now it is Eduardo and Perla Elena who float through the living rooms and hallways, perhaps visiting the still-locked room where no madwoman had ever lived, and only the moans of pain from their mother at the moment of her death and the constant presence of the ghost of General Matias de la Cuesta could be heard.

Now The Madrilera, an imposing and ghostly mansion, is ready to house new memories for young people who, only through photographs, seek to share some moments of Perla Elena and Eduardo's lives. Children search the drawers for letters, cards, and various objects from that time, hoping to validate what their parents had so lovingly told them on rainy nights.

The Three Snakes

When Maria Teresita left for the island of The Three Snakes, she carried with her a sick organism, condemned to the longest agony due to a cancer that had metastasized. Burdened with hatred and poverty, she left behind her family, grandmother and mother, who refused to believe in the cataclysm that threatened them: soup kitchens, ration cards, property expropriation, day and night invasions, interrupted education, altered books, and teachers fearful of being accused of treason by some daring student. Laws that would directly lead to the total loss of freedom of expression and action, under a centralist government that encompassed within its tentacles the institutions responsible for law and order in a country that, like Cambodia and Darfur, would witness massacres and human rights violations.

Terrified, Maria Teresita preferred any other view, so she boarded the 747 that would take her to her new destination: the island of The Three Snakes, sparsely populated by about thirty houses built with wooden planks and the beautiful view of a warm ocean, promising peace for thought and meditation. She enjoyed the first few days drawing sketches of what her surroundings would be like while she lived in the gray, ivy-covered house marked at number 26. The nearest neighbors were a league away, and the sea, with its foamy waves that made her feel dizzy, was her only companion.

On cool nights, nosy mosquitoes pierced her sensitive skin with long stings, leaving her covered in welts that made her increasingly itchy. She had decided to take care of this strange house for a few months. In a briefcase, she carried her most precious books: various literature, some romance novels, and the Bible, a gift from her mother. It was an old Bible, inherited from Grandma Manuela, who had fled the Franco dictatorship, dressed in a long black skirt that she trusted would protect her from the salty sea air. Grandma Manuela kept her Bible and rosary always close at hand. It wasn't a rosary with beads of various sizes to distinguish between the Our Fathers and Hail Mary's; no, this was a small rosary, suitable for a child's hand.

Maria Teresita kept the Bible, but her practical thinking rejected any religious indoctrination, contrary to what she experienced at home, where the atmosphere was austere and faithful to the Holy Scriptures. For her, this was a journey on which she would have the opportunity to form her own opinion about life's events. This wasn't so-called "magical thinking," but rather she was drawn to nature and to certain fantastical tales, where Satan, the Devil, Lucifer, and Mephistopheles alternated in prominence. So many names for a unique being, just hearing them makes her cringe.

Resting from her daily walk, she sat on the dock, watching the ships pass by small boats, ships packed with tourists, large cargo ships perhaps transporting war equipment destined for the Middle East, the setting for so many biblical stories Grandma Manuela had told her, where diverse cultures and religions converge.

"What is your name, miss?" asked a tall, thin man with a sharp nose, whose black cassock blocked the ships she was looking at."

"Maria Teresita," she replied, surprised.

"Oh! Of Saint Teresa of Jesus and the Blessed Virgin Mary. Are you new around here?"

"Yes, I just arrived last week. I don't know a single person, only you, Father."

"My church is on that hill. Attend Mass on Sunday."

"Yes Father," she replied, praying that the lie does not show on her face.

Walking back, she picked up sizable clams and chipi-chipis that slipped through her damp, sandy hands. It would be a delicious dinner, a soup with seafood. House number 26 presented no work at all: small, with two bedrooms, two bathrooms, and a hanging pipe on the terrace that served as a shower for bathers. She completed the cleaning duties quickly, then used the computer in the main room, where she searched for information before venturing out into the surrounding area. She wanted to study the map of the island she inhabited. Using Google and Yahoo, she couldn't locate the island of The Three Snakes, so beautiful but so sparsely populated, and she wondered, why couldn't she find it on the Internet? Was it because it wasn't part of the modern world?

The smell of dead fish permeated the entire house. The soup was ready to be eaten, and after dinner, she retired to her bedroom alone to read and sleep. Already in Morpheus's arms, heavy footsteps on the stairs woke her. Barefoot and wearing a silk robe, she went out to inspect the house, then went back to bed, although she was convinced the noises were coming from the creaking wood of the main staircase.

Months passed with her unwavering routine, strolling along the beach and gazing at the church on the hill. The need to socialize prompted her to visit the church where men, women (some pregnant,) and children crowded the place, while the languid, sharp-nosed priest officiated the rites before the altar. Upon leaving, she noticed that those strange women avoided conversation, so Maria Teresita resolved to attend church services more regularly, seeking to gain the trust of some of them. With great ease, she recited the prayers and followed the ritual, and once back home, she carefully marked the verse they would read the next time.

Slowly, religiosity had become part of her daily life. Walking along the beach, dressed in a black skirt, her Bible hidden in its folds to protect it from the sea salt, she now, like her grandmother Manuela, perceived outdoor activities as sinful, while she continued to hear the strange creaking of the steps at midnight. But she already knew who was making it, and she even anxiously awaited the tall man with a languid figure and sharp nose, from whom, like so many other women in the parish, she was expecting a child.

A story like her grandmother's: an illegitimate son of that rough-headed octopus who so skillfully used the powers his Church conferred upon him: centuries of established hierarchies, enforced chastity that was often violated; sexual abuse of children, committed by priests protected by the institution, always transferring those dark episodes so difficult to forget from parish to parish.

The Dance of the Shadows

The Church of The Three Snakes, with its ramifications of power and abuse, located on that island where Maria Teresita had arrived in search of peace and quiet.

Now with a two-year-old son, out of wedlock, and still pouring holy water on the bed before any sexual contact, fearing pregnancy and praying that temptations would be removed from the place. Now, so close to the devil, incarnated in that languid, sharp-nosed man, in the church doorway, on the island of The Three Snakes, with pointy heads and rattlesnake tails.

Pilgrimage

Rosa is still sick. Despite Teresa turning her over six times a day, there are more sores on her skin. In total despair at not being able to walk, Rosa turns to the unexpected, to the faith her heart dictates, which tells her that only a miracle will get her back on her feet. She went with Teresa to see the Christ on the wall and the Virgin on the hamburger bun. This time, rumors came from the neighboring town, and she believes that, thanks to divine fortune, her bitter tears will slide down the rolling stones, freeing her body of impurities. There will be hope in the air; and if she is cured, she will leave among the rocks of the grotto the list of promises she has yet to keep.

Excited, Teresa pushes her chair up the mound of earth so she can see the threshold where the image of the stream lies.

Teresa, seeing her standing among the red roses and eucalyptus trees, remembers the holy cards she was given as a child. Rosa, alert and opening her eyes ever wider, anxiously seeks to make out the details of her face.

"Teresa, I can't see anything,"

"It's just that she's already vanished. But look there are her feet."

"Teresa, how do you know those are her feet? Besides, you can only see three toes. Does she even have three toes?"

"Oh Rosa, stop being picky. Go on, close your eyes and think that you're going to see her, that it's her, even if you only see her three toes."

Frowning again, Rosa focused on her gaze and said:

"Yes, there she is."

"Did you see her feet?"

"I saw more than that, Teresa. Look: There's the silhouette of her cloak."

"No Rosa, that's the vine."

"Oh no Teresa, now you're the one who doesn't want to see."

Lost in their thoughts, Rosa prays and prays, while Teresa touches the vine and winks at her, declaring that there is no cloak.

The cloudy sky turns dark, and in a fraction of a second, a storm breaks loose.

"Teresa don't go so fast; you'll knock me down. As soon as we arrive, I'll try to get up."

Teresa witnesses the immense effort Rosa makes to stay up.

"Rosa, stop, it's better to rest so we can go sightseeing in the afternoon."

A colonial town with cobblestone streets that wind up and down. The main square is surrounded by stalls displaying religious images for sale. Makeshift food stalls, wafers with burnt milk, cheese, and shredded beef patties. Men, women, and children seeking healing from illnesses and ailments. And others eagerly seeking God.

Today it's this town, tomorrow it will be another, and Teresa will push the wheelchair so Rosa can witness the sacred image and pray for the longed miracle be granted to her.

Airs

Just a few steps away from crossing the sliding door of that New York hospital, Maria Ines was very sure that this would be a short visit, simply to receive a prescription for the medicines that would cure her incipient flu, so common during the winter months. Freezing air seeped through the cracks in the building, air that enveloped passersby in their daily work, and an air of arrogance that made her feel different from the others. She knows that other patients will spend days, weeks, months, and even years battling debilitating illnesses, while she, in a few minutes, would be out of that environment where she did not fit in.

To her surprise, Maria Ines is detained by the doctors, seized by nurses and paramedics. They won't let her go because they don't know what's wrong with her: whether it's not just the flu; whether her arterial blood gas level is low, whether they should consider other possibilities. There will be time to start ruling things out. Blood tubes, arranged in a row, each with a different purpose. Possible causes must be ruled out; the truth must be sought.

Once in the room, seeing the lemon-colored walls, the white bed, and the simple wooden cross hanging at the headboard, Maria Ines felt a sense of welcome and believed that in a few moments she would be protected from the disease. These are moments of reflection, she told herself as she meditated on her life,

Maria Gabriela Madrid

trying to understand what was happening. Electrocardiograms, oxygen level readings, steroids, insulin, narcotics, antibiotics, all together, fought to lower her fever and calm her cough. She was advised to stay in bed, conserving her energy, so scarce lately even for simple activities like brushing her teeth.

The phone rang incessantly. It's family and friends who, concerned about her health, offer moral support. At midday, the sun's rays pass through the glass, marking the moment when she looks through the window and watches with delight and concern the placid flight of a black crow, its wings spread, circling. Surprised to see a crow in the skies of Manhattan, where the most common sight is one of seeing and hearing of pigeons, Maria Ines and her companion laugh somewhat nervously at this unwelcome visitor who brings back memories of her childhood, of watching on the television screen the children rummaging for food scraps in the municipal garbage dump, competing with the vultures flying overhead, vying for the same prey.

Tired, she tries to sleep, squint in and revealing the enormous raccoon-like circles under her eyes. In her sleep, she feels her ragged breathing and counts: one, two, one, two, three, one, two, three, four... and in her sleep, turns around and sees no one. The nurse, upon entering, asks her:

"Is this cross on the floor yours, ma'am?"

"On the floor? But how did it fall, if no one has been behind the headboard?"

Surprised, the nurse places the cross on the bedrail, while Maria Ines closes her eyes and enters the darkness of a disturbing dream where beings dressed in black roam the halls in search of unsuspecting souls to seize. The air is cold, and halls smell of chlorine, common places for so many invisible agents, microbes, bacteria, seemingly insignificant, but which in a short time could send anyone to the afterlife.

Maria Ines's condition has worsened; the electrocardiogram doesn't provide enough information; the doctors' conversations show moments of great tension: whether she's being poisoned; whether the gas exchange isn't appropriate; whether there is more carbon monoxide than oxygen; whether a pulmonary embolism should be ruled out.

At three in the morning, Maria Ines is wheeled on a stretcher to the intensive care unit where they will try to save her. Once the oxygen mask is removed, icy air swirls in a whirlwind of already warm air, having been mixed with the dissipated air of pride. And it wasn't just the flu, it wasn't a short visit, just a short stay where, now with a clear conscience, Maria Ines looks down from above at the hospital bed, at the lemon-colored walls, in search of the wooden cross that never appeared. The black crow takes flight and moves placidly through the air currents of the big city.

Maria Gabriela Madrid

Limbo

Avoiding listening, I covered my ears with my hands, but an inner voice pleaded with me from the depths of my being to continue searching, to read and research, to experience what surrounded me and create my own story. Unfortunately, the rebelliousness of my teenage years didn't allow it. Out of rejection, I sought only to read the frivolous magazines that lay in the wicker baskets scattered in the corners of the bathrooms and living rooms. I sought to fill the void by driving my car along the city's highways, seeking worldly pleasures that would distract me from my true calling, which had been born at nine years old with the creation of children's stories, the only titles I remember: "The Flying Squirrel," "Aymara-Aymara," and "My Blind Friend."

The stories, kept in a box hidden in the closet, accumulated like images flowing from my memory, which I learned to discard, setting aside without knowing why. They were images that, for moments, began the process of weaving the story together, threading together characters, situations, dreams, desires, and fears that would eventually become part of the stories. Unfortunately, the heavy box is no longer with me. It was in that month of August that I lost half of my being. That evening witnessed how I was separated from the stories that reflected, through my eyes as a child, adolescent, and woman, the reality that surrounded me.

"Maria Andreina," is what my mother often calls me whenever we can't reach an agreement, and she always advises me: "stop being a pagan and seek, through baptism, the passport to access the kingdom of God."

Refusing to allow any religious indoctrination, I listened only to my conscience, until one August afternoon, late at night, I thought of my mother's words telling me: "Maria Andreina, don't come back late." But that day, as I picked up the box of stories, I was lost in a memory, or an illusion, and while trying to fix it in my memory, I distracted myself by trying to cross the tracks of the freight train that in an instant took over my life.

Now in limbo, I walk through the ruined train station, with its white stone arches, arabesques on the embroidered concrete pillars culminating in a central rose window with its uniform petals that decorate the station's columns. The walls, with their cracked paint falling to pieces, are evidence that the days of great splendor are far behind us. The trains arriving are no longer heard, nor the hurried footsteps of passengers. Now everything is still, silent, in an atmosphere of peace, while I, Maria Andreina, wander in search of any soul to talk to.

The icy wind seeps through the cracks in the walls, while I watch the hours pass without being able to return.

Now I see children running around, pagan souls like me, who never had the chance to know Jesus. Limbic beings who were not taken to the baptismal font; mortal sin that was not cleansed by baptism. Limbo that soothes the anguish of parents whose children left without that initial cleansing and death itself sent them to the limbo they are now trying to erase. Wandering through the station, I wonder, where will we go if this structure collapses? While my weeping mother calls me, and everyone surrounds my coffin and prays for the salvation of my soul.

Heaven or Hell?

I always longed to grow up. To grow physically, intellectually, emotionally, and spiritually; but it wasn't until I met Horacio that something gave me the strength and showed me the path to pursue my dreams, so different from those of Jose, my husband. He, so methodical, always eager to explain everything. I, magical, and with a loyalty that lasted until I found Horacio, crazy like me, wandering with no known destination. With the sole desire to share our mutual passion, Horacio listened to my theories about life, about relativity: "It's relative, in this world, everything is temporary." But it wasn't like that for Jose, who already had the coffins ready, one next to the other: his black and mine pink, a pale pink, as death should be, almost toneless, like oblivion.

The fact is that in this life, those who survive no longer remember those who die, leaving only traces in the memories of those who knew them. These were memories that, over the years, could be distorted and even idealized, as happened with my friend Sofia, with whom I shared so many experiences. Years after her death, I barely retain the memory of a few anecdotes and the fear that, with the passage of time, nothing more than her name will remain in my memory. I try to remember the climbs up the university stairs, the patties with cheese we ate in the mornings in the cafeteria before entering class. I remember the frenzy caused by those who called us to ask us out. We often exchanged phone numbers: the one with curly hair for you and the blond one for me. Giggle laughter that not even our mothers understood, until one fateful afternoon, the agony began for Sofia, and she could barely climb the stairs because she tired easily; and between doctor's appointments and treatments, in just one year, Death took her, at only twenty-two years old. And I, now thirty-eight years old, I still miss her.

I wish she could see my life and I could see hers. I wish we could share more anecdotes, but Death is unforgiving. Will she come wearing a long, black dress? Or is it a short circuit in our system, and our brains are tangling with images and experiences to make the transition more pleasant? Always terrified, Aunt Eulalia called me a heretic. Until one day, driving her car in the middle of a storm, she lost the brakes, and when she couldn't stop, her growing anxiety drove her into a state of panic that prevented her from seeing the street she was driving down. She only noticed images of her childhood: My grandmother Berta (her mother) hitting her and punishing her in the bathroom for throwing her favorite magazines into the ravine.

What about the memories of Aunt Eulalia? Always anguished, as if they were part of the hell that awaited her. These weren't just pleasant memories, and to brighten the mood, she was now sacrificing herself for others. Her personal interests took a back seat: she no longer painted or wrote; she only cleaned and cooked to please her sisters. Did she believe she was winning heaven? Could she teach her posthumous destiny: heaven or hell? That's how Aunt Eulalia lived, and on the day, she died, those present at the funeral couldn't stop wondering how her aunt had forgotten that the cleaning fluid was for the toilet and had drunk it. The chemicals she'd ingested had turned her skin blue, and her prominent teeth stood out in a forced smile.

The family and friends who attended the funeral never spoke of the void Aunt Eulalia left behind. They told stories of old times, and while some enjoyed the soup and crackers, others commented on the mourners' outfits. Aunt Eulalia's body wasn't an object of curiosity for those present. No one came close to seeing her. The fear of the other world prevented any approach. Aunt's dress was red and blue as she was, the color of the dress placed her in another reality, or so her mother believed, an admirer of Egyptian culture who intended to put the cat in the coffin, place bowls of food, and place the photo of Aunt Eulalia's only love, who, terrified by the marriage plans, took to the road and never returned.

My first encounter with death was heartbreaking. Then came the dreams that were buried in time and that I now try to revive. I'm going to meet Horacio this week in the alley at San Vicente and Alarcon. Will I see him changed? Will I feel the same as before? That intimidating feeling and the desire to be by his side, who knows? But at least now I can see myself living here in my own heaven and hell. I know that was what Sofia felt, who, in just three months, and without any explanation, was fulfilling her most hidden dreams, such as traveling to the Bat Cave to observe the life of bats, living beings in complete darkness. She also called Efrain and while she was drawing his portrait, between canvases and brushes fulfilled her most ardent desired: the promise that Efrain would keep the parrot "Eustaquio," and the tablecloths she had embroidered with so much effort that they planned to share in their married life. Now, in my sadness and joy, I live the days, the hours, minutes and seconds of this existence, right or wrong, which, over the years, with my own death, will simply dissipate.

Decisions

The time had come. She had to decide, and Grandma's advice had so earnestly repeated echoed in her mind: "Alfonsina, don't worry, have the children God sends you, and there will always be help to raise them!" Not to mention those raised alone, under the care of the nanny on duty. To this end, Grandma Mariela made sure the nanny was well-educated, not one of those who might bring bad habits. Following Grandma Mariela's advice on raising her children, Alfonsina was already pregnant for the sixth time, and by the third month of pregnancy, she had overcome the normal discomforts of carrying a foreign being in her womb. No more nausea or vomiting, now only that swollen belly that would enclose the new being for a few months.

The medical checkup revealed a myriad of concerns: that the baby might be mentally challenged, that it might have some deformity. They advised her to terminate the pregnancy, to avoid the suffering of giving birth to a being who wouldn't be able to function in the world. "But why? Alfonsina wondered. We'll get her a full-time nurse. I'm sure Carmela would take care of her. Could we pay her more? Right, Gustavo?" But Gustavo didn't even speak; all he said was that whatever she decided would happen. The decision of life or death would depend on her. Grandma Mariela, clinging to the Bible, assured them that God would change that fate, and for the following months prayed, prayed and prayed.

No more medical tests, no more attachment to this new being that the nanny promised to care for. She would try not to see her, better yet, avoid meeting her. It would be very painful for her and for that overly hardworking father, who, just by looking at her, would remember and admit that something defective had come into the world from her womb. Living in a society that celebrates perfection rather than the human being as such, a society where beauty standards emphasize the lack of tolerance for those who fall short of the ideal, a society where there are always those who seek out butchers to make them look better, more acceptable at least.

Alfonsina and her husband preferred not to face the situation that awaited them. They knew that no surgeon would be able to accommodate something so imperfect. And with prayer and prayer, the day arrived. A C-section was scheduled in the clinic that was equipped with the latest technology. There would be no camera or video recorder. There would be nothing beautiful to remember, only parents' anxiousness to be rid of that 'strange bundle'. A young mother, obscure in her own eyes and good in the eyes of others, only she knew of the rejection of this sixth child that was about to arrive, and she couldn't wait to end the ordeal. All she saw in this fragile, unborn daughter were the thousand and one complications; and above all, the dreaded disease.

While the doctors tried to stabilize the baby, Gustavo and Alfonsina prayed and prayed, asking for her to die, praying for a natural death. Not even the nanny wanted to be with her anymore. Seeing her in the intensive care unit made her nauseous, and she impulsively gave up caring for her.

"What do I do with her now?" Alfonsina wondered.

Gustavo, isolated, repeated: "I'll find the money, but those children are yours, and you have to be with them."

Desperate, she saw that the baby was not what she and her husband might have imagined; she was a broken mirror, a distorted figure, never made in the image and likeness of her parents.

Alfonsina continued praying, but this time she prayed more to the devil, to the demon, to the angels of death, to anyone who would listen, always holding the black rosary in her hand, trying not to let anyone notice that it was the same demon to whom she was praying for a fatal end. Many were the nights she sat in a chair near the maternity ward. They were nights clutching the black rosary, praying for the newborn to leave this earthly place. Close relatives, avoiding facing the problem, made phone calls, offering her unconditional support: "Pray, ask God that she will be saved." But "Kill her, kill her, kill her", were the voices that Alfonsina heard, coming from her mind in her most desperate moments.

It was those intrusive voices that wouldn't let her think, and which she heard with increasing insistence, that led her that night, at the most opportune moment, to pull the cord and, feigning desperation, run in search of the help that, fortunately for her, she knew wasn't going to come.

She would pretend to cry for several days, choose the coffin, already paid for before the birth, and after the funeral everything would return to normal, and it would be time to hide the black rosary, the time to leave the devil aside because then, with their five children, they would once again be the exemplary family!

Cats

When Carlos was transferred to China, the first thing he thought was this would be an enriching experience and that it would open the doors to a different culture. With great excitement, he moved with his wife and daughter to Beijing, a city of a thousand faces, a culture long established, and a population uniformed in blue suits even at the end of the second millennium. Entire generations were battered, where intellectuals (writers, schoolteachers, and university professors) were sent to distant villages to work the land, harvest rice, tend farms, sow seeds, or any other activity that distanced them from their intellectual status. Many preferred to die in the face of such humiliation.

Upon their arrival, they were placed in the foreigners' ghetto. Among the thousands of recommendations, they were advised not to date Chinese women, considered sacred, untouchable like the Egyptian cats that had arrived in Asia. Orange, grayish, and black cats like the hair of Siang-Hui, a young twenty-something, daughter of General Shuiya. The party offered exquisite dishes: Kung Pao shrimp, mushroom lo mein, and, among others, exquisite coral and jade prawns, like Shiang-Hui's attire. She wore a long coral gown and a yellow jade ornament around her slender neck, adding to the splendor of the room.

Carlos's wife, invisible to him, was no obstacle to his approach to the young woman. He couldn't hide such an overwhelming attraction. Like cats, independent, self-centered, and oblivious to everything happening around them, they found a way to be together. Interesting and cultured, Shiang-Hui captivated him, so they escaped and hid in the narrow corridors and made love. She, feline, delicate, with her claw-like nails, left the mark of her passion on Carlos's sweaty back. He, ardent and aggressive, without waiting for her to be ready, like a cat with its thorny penis, if pulled out too soon, scratches the female cat, who angrily turns around to bite the daring man.

Some nights, meows of disappointment could be heard, and other times, shrieks of pleasure betrayed them. Months later, a snitch followed them under the moonlight and trying to curry favor with Shiang Hui's father, handed him compromising photos. Faced with the evidence, the General, overcome with rage, kidnapped Carlos for weeks. His wife and daughter missed him, while Shiang Hui, trying to save his life, promised her father never to see Carlos again, while trying to hide the being growing in her womb and, like an orange cat, sucking the nutrients to feed her young.

The General, ashamed, tried to convince her to have an abortion; otherwise, he would sacrifice her to avoid humiliation.

Fleeing like a feline, Shiang-Hui escaped the uniformed men stationed in the corridors, searching for any clue to betray her. She had decided on motherhood. She would defend it until the final meow, experiencing the heartbreaking pain of the birth of a new being, while Carlos, with his destiny marked, drawn in the stars and in the embossed sky that warned him of what would happen to him, once his mission in China was complete, returned with his wife and daughter to his homeland.

Little Green Eyes

Rocking in the wicker chair, Clara, exasperated, feels the nightstand for the third time in search of her glasses. Hurriedly, she turns on the light, gets dressed, and quickly leaves to catch the train.

It will be a day like so many others. She'll walk the same streets, see the same shop windows, drink coffee, and lock herself in the cubicle where she'll make phone calls until six. She'll look for clients, anticipating rejection when she offers a product that has expired.

It will be just another day in the tedious routine, and letting out a sigh, she wonders: "Where is the city of skyscrapers, the limitless city where any fantasy becomes reality?"

Tired, she doesn't even stop to remember her dreams. She walks quickly to catch the first train car. Before getting on, she doesn't know what's wrong; she feels an obligation, an uncontrollable desire to offer help because there's a blind man standing on the platform, and she's worried that he won't be able to get on the train alone.

"Listen: you're here, just take three steps forward. I'll let you know as soon as the doors open."

"Thank you, but it's not necessary. Get in and let the minutes fly by. Don't rush to get there. Look, I'm selling this, but I'm giving it to you."

Putting it in her purse, Clara gets on the train and, amidst the smells and sweat, she waits for someone to get up and sit down.

Curious, she opens the package and, astonished, sees that it's a pair of contact lenses, the opposite of the thick-lens glasses that damage the septum of her nose daily.

Motivated, she renews her wardrobe and every morning she puts on her "green eyes."

Contact with that foreign body is permanent. The watery liquid on the gelatinous body requires daily care. In the morning, she'll have to shake them before putting them in, and at night, moisten them to store them until the next day. With "green eyes," Clara learned to stop. Every day she walks the same streets and sees the same shop windows, but now she observes her surroundings, listens to the birds chirping, and she raises her gaze to the sky to see the end of the skyscrapers. The joy of living has returned to her body; it's the magical city that transmits the energy of being here and now.

Adjusting her skirt and cashmere sweater, she entered Rolando's office, her new boss, to ask for a promotion.

As soon as the boss saw her, he looked her over from head to toe, focusing on the curly reddish hair that falls over her shoulders. He, with his black eyes and few eyelashes, winked, flirting with the strange little green eyes. Without taking his eyes off her, he gave her a new position within the company.

"You'll be my personal secretary."

Standing, with her legs shaking, Clara accepted and was glad she was wearing boots, as they prevented the boss from noticing her nervousness.

He senses it. It's going to be a romance.

"I know she'll say yes," he repeats to himself.

That same afternoon, they went to lunch near the river. Waiting to board the train that would take them back to the office, Clara pointed out the blind man on the platform to Rolando, who in a flash, chatting with a stranger, took a baseball ball from his pocket. Astonished, they watched as the stunned young man accepted the ball and, climbing into the cab, shouted that he would play for Sunday's team.

Sunday in which Clara and Rolando watched the game. The moment when the ball soared through the air and fell in front of the yellow taxi, which would run over the distracted young baseball player. Clara, to avoid seeing it, closed her eyes tightly, unaware that the watery liquid would escape from the contact lenses and weave cobwebs that would leave her in the shadows. Intertwined magic circulating on the winds of the big city.

Ritual

I never thought the popular saying, "small town, big hell," could apply so accurately to North Carolina. Miguel Antonio had been transferred by the banana company where he worked to a new division, this one a tobacco company. The plane we were traveling on, although battered by the storm, finally managed to land. Once in the car, we traveled through a bucolic, cloudy, smoky-white landscape, where only trees could be seen on either side in all their splendor. Nothing moved, only the car moving in search of our new home.

The apartment complexes we visited made me feel such a strong sense of oppression that I was sure I couldn't live there. We moved three times in three days, until we arrived at a complex with a clearer view where the adjacent trees were far enough apart to not block our view. While Miguel Antonio spent his time immersed in his work, I explored the surroundings during the day.

The locals, with their distinctive accents, were overly friendly and generous, and so were the people from other parts who, like me, had come with a purpose: some attracted by a new job; others, younger, eager to start college; or doctors who were sleepless, always wandering around, as if they were on another planet.

In North Carolina, there are places like Durham-Chapel Hill, teeming with universities, most notably Duke University and North Carolina University (UNC); several shopping malls; and Cary, a tech hub. There was also The Park, named for the expanse of restricted land designated for the development of research projects and companies like Glaxo Smith-Kline, Bayer, IBM, Techno Cary, and the city of Raleigh, the capital, where government offices like the State House and the Capitol are located; beautiful parks and lakes everywhere, and the most international of all, the park dedicated to Sarah Duke, wife of the tycoon whose family had donated money for the construction of Duke University.

It was a park populated by exotic trees and plants brought from all over the world. The star in the middle of the park displayed the name Sarah Duke, accompanied by a loving dedication. Many said that Sarah lay there, her ghost admiring the flowers during long nighttime walks. Often, in my solitude, the coming of night would set my imagination soaring, and I would wonder: who was behind that tree? How many bodies were buried among so much greenery? I knew the history of those lands, which had belonged first to the Native Americans, then to European settlers, and finally to a mixed-race group that was gradually taking them over. But above all, I was intrigued by the feeling of fear that struck me every time I looked at the immense pines.

Those wide and beautiful trees held secrets! I shared an increasingly limited amount of time with Miguel Antonio, and that April afternoon, he noticed I was strange, different. Distracted by his long-winded rhetoric, I was just trying to run out to visit Florencia again, a local woman I had met at the mall who told me stories of those places. That afternoon, she told me about the fire that had once consumed the store. As if in a trance, Florencia, obeying only her recollections, began

105

shouting at the people, urging them to leave. Apparently, only I was listening. No one came forward to help her. Finally, I managed to calm her with a hot tea that, I was sure, would put her to sleep.

Years passed, and my gatherings with Florencia continued. The social events, now at their peak, were the setting for the few moments shared with Miguel Antonio. The beautiful halls, mostly colonial venues in the southern style, high-ceilinged houses with plaster moldings and marquetry on the wide central staircases. I imagined what the mansions of Charleston, that Southern port ruined by the Civil War, would have looked like. The port, which in its prime had been the center of commerce, the cotton plantations, the tired slaves, dominated by the whip to ensure greater yield, the nightly tales of white and black magic, and enlivening the endless days, the sad songs, whose rhythms, over time, became blues.

In Charleston, white girls were always bathed and dressed by the slaves. The mansions were decorated with the greatest splendor, decorations brought from India and Africa, and German eggshell porcelain tableware. All that luxury that during the Civil War no more ships would arrive at the port and trade would end, leaving only the luxurious tableware without food and everyone would witness how the owners and their families died of hunger. What would I have given to be able to exchange any of those luxury belongings for a loaf of bread? But there I was, at a party in North Carolina, after landing from that astral trip to Charleston.

Exhausted, Miguel Antonio suggested going home. He was tired, and I was more awake than ever!

Could I possibly run into Florencia? Could I possibly invite her at that early hour?

Overcoming my fears, I crossed the street and entered the dark, violent black forest. I couldn't see anything, I could only hear some uhm mm! like Yogis or Hare Krishnas.

I approached slowly and spotted Florencia, surrounded by strangers. I could see them dancing and singing because the circle was dimly lit by a bonfire and perhaps helped by the light of the moonlight, I noticed something strange about their torn clothes, their gaunt faces and their languid figures. They were all moving towards me.

Now I understood that fire that Florencia had told me about, that fire that had devoured those who were judiciously working rolling the tobacco leaves and that tobacco factory whose doors were chained to prevent them from escaping.

This place, now a shopping center, once housed almost the entire town. One hundred people had perished amidst screams and wailing!

The terror gripped me. It was an overwhelming sensation and once inside the circle surrounded by Florencia and others in an instance they consumed my living flesh. Now in the moonlight I looked putrefied among the trees that had caused me so much anguish. And to think that this would now be the path to follow: Always in search of someone good, to become the owner of one more soul that would be lost in the vicinity of hell!

I returned to the house to prevent Miguel Antonio from noticing my absence and knowing that this town would be my final resting place.

The Dance of the Shadows

Small town, big hell! Locals who, like Florencia and I, were hopelessly trapped.

Maria Gabriela Madrid

Ancestral Basement

"What's going on? what's going on?" Alfredo shouted. His house of cards is collapsing! His wife of twenty years wants to say goodbye. He'll be alone, without his two pre-adolescent children and the brown-coated Afghan hound. Mariana has had to deal with his destructive habits for many years now. It's not just the drunkenness and the absences from important events; it's also witnessing this stranger who takes over his entire being and, on top of that, is violent, always abusing those around him. His sons, Rafael and Andrés, fear him every time he touches the bottle, and that night, like so many others, he returned to the air-conditioned basement where the wine cellar invites him to open the French bottle to unburden his sorrows. He needs to repair the central air conditioning. It's clogged, and the air remains at the frigid temperature of the cellars.

Wrapped in a thick yellow wool sweater, Alfredo sat around the round oak table. The dim light lures him along winding paths, imagining what Roman tunnels and catacombs must have looked like. Being passionate about history and a Professor of Comparative Religions, on sabbatical, without the worry of preparing classes, only with the task of packing and traveling with his family to Italy, he staggered to the floor to sleep a few hours before packing. Transported back in time, he relived the last lecture he gave before starting his sabbatical: The Roman Empire, the persecutions of

Christians for not submitting to the worship of Caesar. Christians punished with death for worshipping only their God, (Father-Son-Holy-Spirit).

Anticipating the trip to Italy, Alfredo dreamed of those tunnels, of the catacombs where tourists visit the altars, pray, and commemorate the deaths of the martyrs whose names are inscribed on the rock walls. Fearful, he dreams of hiding so as not to be caught. His weaknesses and his failed marriage are what torment him the most. Mariana decided to push him out of her life, but she won't divorce him. Her pettiness makes her want everything for herself and she knows that her children, who detest him for so many years of abuse, will cooperate with her until the end.

Like the martyrs, in the days of the catacombs, who felt their necks severed, Alfredo, semi-conscious, feels the sharp axe penetrating his skin. Heart-rending screams of pain that no one hears, because he's in that cold basement surrounded by bottles that as witness with smiling faces are all around him. He feels like he's dying, but he wants to believe he's in the midst of a violent nightmare. A dream from which he'll never wake up, and, like the martyrs, he knows he's dying in that cold, though modern, concrete tunnel. And all for power, the power to control, the power of money that Mariana now wants for herself and her children.

Drunk, fallen, and unable to defend himself, he looked at Mariana, Rafael, and Andres sending him one last message, while his dismembered body will remain in one of the cellars. Because he's on sabbatical, no one will ask about him. They will think he disappeared on the trip. A timely trip for Mariana to collect the insurance money that will empower his three great loves, always smiling until the end.

New York...! Manhattan...! New York...!

New York, Manhattan, New York! A city of multiple cultures, idiosyncrasies, yearnings... New York, a city of searching and exotic pleasures, savored by the finest palates. The New York of Fifth Avenue, Madison Square Garden, Park Avenue... Ambition, the power of money, ambiguity, brands... New York, just a facade! ... Dresses, shoes, bags. New York so different from that of ideals, populated by bohemians and painters. SOHO, now commercial. Expensive. Exclusive galleries and restaurants. And Greenwich Village, so eager to find its identity. Writers, gays, musicians, and rappers... Heroin, marijuana, cocaine. The senses are heightened only to land violently...

That's how Ada lived. Ada, a theater artist, a bohemian, so talented in the New York of impudence. Free sex without complications. Life to the fullest... Ada, full of dreams and challenges, until that afternoon, after her current boyfriend had left, she found her cocktail in the shadowy alley. A cocktail of mixed and altered heroin that would plunge her into that unfathomable abyss. Her excitement turned into an acute anguish for breathing, already altered by the asthma medication. Her racing, galloping heart stopped in a final burst.

New York, where passersby and tourists break the monotony, sometimes yearning for, sometimes idealizing, the surrounding reality. The outdated romanticism of the Empire State Building... Cultural New York: Universities, Art Centers, Shows, Conferences, Theater, Opera, Ballet, African Rhythmic Movements, Drums, Taiko Masala, Japan... Ethnic groups intermingled on an afternoon of pleasure, Washington Square: a confusion of smells, sweat, tired people, moving back and forth. Africa. Thailand. Japan... Rhythms, music, melodies, music, colorful costumes, music, joy everywhere!

African American Harlem. Latin Harlem. Tarentines. Vegetable stands. Shops... Intellectual New York! Movie theaters, oratories, conversations, the why of it all; the why of I don't know what... Intense exchange of ideas and opinions. Explosion in intellectual New York... Colorful New York! New York of Times Square! In times past, it was riddled with brothels, and now, with avant-garde theaters. Commercial theater. Lights. Advertisements. Multicolored banners. Endless curiosities. Museums galore...

New York! The city of eternally lit lights. Lights that recall that fateful day at the World Trade Center. More than two thousand souls were extinguished, and today, the sky illuminated, and the excavations continue. New York of suffering! Of hard life, of endless work, of daily struggle.

New York of traditions! Chinatown. Little Italy. Religious traditions. Jews! Orthodox Jews. Muslims. Christians. New York! Frivolous New York!

Vibrant and thoughtful New York! Exciting and beloved New York!... New York!

Threads

In the 21st century, Beatriz turns thirty-three years old on that April afternoon, the age of Christ. An important age at which she hopes to find fulfillment both professionally and romantically. Unfortunately, her boyfriend of nine years never asked the long-awaited question, and the night before, during a simple argument over who would take the dog for a walk, heated tempers escalated to the point of no return and then plummeted into the abyss. A feeling of emptiness that both already felt from having been involved in a relationship on the verge of collapse.

Beatriz works from 9 a.m. to 3 p.m. as an assistant in a dental office. In her free time, she makes Guatemalan-style baskets for a business she's trying to establish, which would give free rein to the artistic side of her personality. Brightly colored threads and pastel shades. Thick threads. Unlike the delicate dental floss, which penetrates so many strange mouths. Intricate spaces where she seeks to remove the tartar left by improper brushing. Threads she controls like the Lord himself, and no event or circumstance escapes him. Threads with which he manipulates the puppets that inhabit this planet, like the twelve marionettes that decorate the office. Small, medium, and large puppets made of papier-mâché, placed in a semicircle on her desk.

A recent dentistry graduate, Braulio takes care of

every detail in his office and obsessively seeks perfection. That afternoon, wanting to acquire canine, mare, and even coyote jaws, he asked Beatriz to accompany him to collect them. It seemed like an attractive idea to add the jaws of cadavers from the university laboratory to the decor. Unfortunately for him, only anatomy students had access to the cadavers. That afternoon he drove an hour to the cliff where the Solar house, belonging to the Department of Natural Sciences, is located.

The house, built with natural materials, has walls covered with newspaper, finally painted white, supporting the panels on the roof that filtered solar energy. The septic tanks had deep tunnels to prevent unpleasant odors due to the lack of running water. Only he knew that downstairs, in the basement connected to the tunnels, there was a tank full of excrement that, through the appropriate process, was converted into fertilizer for the plants.

In the laboratory, on the countertops, they kept stuffed animals: the head of a moose, a coyote with a dove in its jaws, and faceless jaws waiting to fulfill their function. Braulio would place those teeth at the entrance of his office, some in constant anachronism, others in harmony. Beatriz's teeth gave him the creeps, so Braulio always tried to avoid her, but that afternoon he needed her to help him carry his precious luggage.

Beatriz, always short of money, couldn't afford the proper treatment to offer a perfect smile, but that afternoon was the moment. Braulio's nervous tics began to manifest; pulling out his hair was no longer enough to calm him; his leg was constantly moving, his gaze fixed on the yellow pile of teeth driving him mad.

The rope within his reach made the process easier. He attacked Beatriz from behind, tying her to the black chair at the central counter. Her screams would not be heard. Lost in thought, he paid attention only to the water running down the cliff. Without any prior anesthesia, he grabbed the strands of rope holding her and, at every opportunity, inserted them into Beatriz's mouth, causing blood to flow out and eventually mix with the tears rolling down her cheeks, while an inner voice ordered Braulio to pull them out. He took the pliers and began pulling out the teeth, whose final destination would be the showroom of his practice. Inside the glass vitrine, they would be clean, shiny, and free of tartar, contrary to the final fate of Beatriz's corpse: the excrement deposit that awaits her, to one day return to the planet and become fertilizer for the plants surrounding the solar-powered residence. Late at night, under the moonlight, Braulio looks with pleasure that his assistant's smile has finally been fixed.

Maria Gabriela Madrid

Salome!

Jean Paul Pascal loved being at the cutting edge of fashion. His suits, made by Galliano and Yves Saint Laurent, were in his closet, waiting to be chosen for the next day. As a financial analyst, he always carried his iPhone and iPod. His favorite music was classical, but that afternoon, bewildered by his dismissal, the only thing floating around in his head were the words of his department head: "Jean Paul, you know we appreciate you and we know how valuable you are, but we have to let you go."

In a state of shock, Jean Paul wandered the streets of the financial district. Merrill Lynch's powerful bull now looked like a scrawny ox, and his delicate hands were no longer warmed by his cashmere gloves. The icy wind seeped through his bones like a sharp knife. Tired and hungry, he saw an unassuming coffee place where neon lights announced Salome's arrival from Spain.

"Sir, for a tiny sum, Salome as a fortune-teller will foresee your future." A twelve-year-old girl stationed at the door of the establishment told him.

Jean Paul agreed, and guided by the girl, went to a small, dark, windowless room, where the only lighting was four brightly colored bulbs embedded in each corner.

Jean Paul imagined the Salome of the fairy tales, that exotic gypsy with cinnamon-colored skin, long curly hair, and jet-black eyes, who would be waiting for him, seated with a mysterious gaze amidst silks and brocades, like a painting by Henri Regnault, resting her bare feet on the Persian carpet brought from the Ottoman Empire. Jean Paul was convinced he would see the Salome of his dreams, the one possessed of a magical aura from traveling back and forth to the afterlife.

He placed his jacket on the circular table, along with the two electronic devices. The floral fabric of the tablecloth reminded him of the plain of daisies that bloom around the Hudson River in the summer.

Peeking out, Jean Paul felt a gust of icy wind as Salome's long, weathered hand drew the floral curtain toward the left side of the column. Wide-eyed, Jean Paul anticipated seeing Salome's face and saw that she was not beautiful, but acceptable, not to say unpleasant. And she was not young, more like a ripe fruit about to fall. The lines on Salome's face were not smooth but rather furrows that were overly made up. Jean Paul was terrified when he saw her, but in a split second he remembered that she was there to read his delicate hand.

She was toothless, he was not. She wore thick-framed glasses, he did not. She dressed in rags, he did not. She had a place to live, he soon would not.

The apartment where he lives belongs to the company, and he has the rest of the week to vacate it. He spent the salary earned during his short weeks of employment furnishing his bedroom, living room, and dining room. He also spent it buying suits, shoes, accessories, and paying for the trips and lunches he shared with his coworkers, who, like him, were recent college graduates. It was appearances, appearances, and appearances, and now Jean Paul owes even his gait.

Still absorbed in his problems, he heard Salome whistling the song of the fallen and asking him to extend his left hand. Salome took his hand and brought it closer to her face. Jean Paul felt her hot breath and imagined it fogging up the line of life, of work, of heart. Salome took off her glasses, blew on the lenses, and with the tip of her green shirt wiped away the excess moisture.

"Look, young man, you're overwhelm."

"What do you mean?"

"How did you get so far into debt? You won't have a job for a long time, and a mature woman will help you get back on your feet."

"Tell me more, tell me more…"

"Return what you bought this week, give up the apartment, and you'll see how you'll find a place to live. The place I see here is small, with neon lights."

"What else do you see? What else?"

"I see that they'll steal your jacket and your electronic devices, and I see that love will save you from wandering the streets."

"Say no more, woman," Jean Paul said, and getting up, he took his jacket, his two electronic devices, and walked toward Central Park.

Time passed, and Jean Paul experienced what the fortune teller had predicted. Without an apartment, he slept in the parks. Desperate, he put his possessions up for sale; but he didn't get enough money to buy the ticket that would take him back to France. And his girlfriend, the one who among so many beautiful young women managed to stay by his side through good times, now, through bad times, packed her bags and left, because an unemployed man like Jean Paul didn't deserve to be her partner.

Only the night witnessed the endless walks through the city. He sleeps in Central Park precisely on the sidewalk under the bridge to shelter from the rain and listens day after day to the evening songs that once brought him joy but now filled him with dread, reminding him that time was passing, and he was still out of work and wandering the streets.

Disoriented and tired, he walked blocks and blocks with a lost look, and without noticing the road, surprised he stopped in front of the business with neon lights and remembering the prediction of Salome, he entered the establishment in search of the woman who months before read his hand.

Jean Paul, dizzy from not having eaten and hot, began to suffocate, and with gasping breath, one, two, one, two, three, he knew he was short of breath. Untying his tie, he leaned against the circular table while he put down his jacket and two electronic devices.

Suddenly and without warning, he felt a weakness in his legs, falling, lying on the ground. The niece's cries warned Salome of what had happened, so she, dusting off the vase of roses and orange blossoms, prepared the potion that would wake him up.

"Auntie, look, I already have his jacket and gadgets. Don't give him the potion, he's not going to give you money."

"Yes Mija, but it will give me other things that you are not ready to understand."

Icy gusts, smells of jasmine and fresh cherries flooded the air. Salome brought him the potion. Taking it in his hands, Jean Paul inhaled the scent of jasmine flowers, while together, they bit into the juicy cherries feeling an indescribable sensation of fullness.

Hot and cold air blinded the black eyes and the eyes behind the thick pair of glasses, allowing the differences and defects to be ignored. Haunted environment where the found souls merged into one.

Woman in Tyrolean Suit

The compound impregnated by cigarette smoke, the desks located opposite each other without dividing walls, a workplace with cups of coffee everywhere, tired men and women, sometimes with the impetus to work although on many occasions the restlessness, disillusionment and corruption of the system, put a stop to Tom's determination to discover the truth.

He had been working as a crime scene photographer for some time. The suspiciously guarded evidence was captured in the brightly colored photos. Blood, human pain, cruelty to fellow human beings and animals is something that inexplicably touched the most sensitive fibers of his being.

Father of three daughters, at night, in an annex of his apartment in Washington Square, Tom photographs beauty in all its splendor. Women and girls eager to have a portfolio to show to advertising agencies. As a photographer, now in full swing from classified ads in the city's most widely circulated newspaper, Tom has a clientele that is bringing in more money than he did as a judicial police photographer.

His wife Herminia, with thirteen years of living together, is already tired of the routine, the monotony that her life has become and the bedroom problems that contribute to her feeling more isolated every day. Determined to leave him, one afternoon she left with the three Marias, her daughters.

Now lonely and sheltered in his work, Tom finishes his work later and later. The crime of that May afternoon left him shocked, unable to sleep. It was a young girl of just 12 years old who was lying in a fetal position in the vicinity of the park located in front of his building.

Criminality was approaching his home. Absorbed in the evidence, he thinks about how it happened. The young woman half-naked, surrounded by white lilies and yellow daisies and a black butterfly in the concave space of her chest. Who could have done it? This was a neighborhood inhabited by hard-working and respectable families. Obsessed, he drew up several hypotheses: Had she been killed elsewhere and then her body thrown out in the open? Would it have happened in a building near his? What would be the long-awaited answer? Stephanie, the victim, was not his neighbor and the police had no idea of where she came from.

Months passed and nothing new emerged. Alone and with no one to claim her, Stephanie's body was decomposing in the morgue in the center of the capital and everything pointed to it being another cold case that would bulge the folders of the offices on the fifth floor.

In Tom's photography room, with rustic floors and photos of the grateful aspiring models, long work sessions take place between him, the model on duty and that intruding woman who always accompanies him through his window. A stout woman spinning, while Tom watches her for hours always turning in the bakery across de street. Butterfly-shaped honey cakes are his favorites. The woman in Tyrolean dress, with a lot of color, shows how lilies and daisies adorn her dress, while she turns,

turns and turns, like her mother who as a child took him to the brothel to witness her dances and the hours passed while she danced around the tube.

Absorbed and with a blank stare, Tom remembered how she turned and turned until a soft knock on the door of his study alerted him. It was Maria, a seventeen-year-old girl who came for the advertisement in the newspaper. Disturbed by memories, he began the photographic session. Under the table was the torn leather bag with sharp knives, Super Knives. Crazy, he sees the knives, he sees Maria, he presses the button on the Kodak camera: click, click, click... and more and more his gaze escapes to contemplate the robust and colorful woman who turns, turns and turns.

He turns off the camera and wielding the knife he pounces on Maria. The swan neck, white as snow, is dyed by rivers of warm blood. Red, purple, black, blood gushes from the carotid artery, essential for life. Without much resistance, the young woman's anguished gaze slowly faded, unlike his, enraged and triumphant is determined to focus on the robust woman in the colorful Tyrolean costume who turned, turned and turned.

21st Century Woman

The meeting is scheduled. It will take place in a year and Rosario Altamirano can already feel the butterflies fluttering against the walls of her stomach. This time it will be different; this time she will prepare to show off her best. In this century that is beginning, the advances in medicine will serve to provide her with sure success. She only must follow the advice of Aunt Hortensia to look like her: full and sensual lips achieved through the miraculous Botox, and the body with a silhouette that is not Venusian, because in these times the bones must point out of the skin to show a perfect bone structure.

Aunt Hortensia has all the secrets: "Daughter, never go to bed with your makeup on. You should use night cream, day cream, eye cream, and sunscreen." But Rosario required something more, she had the precise time for liposuction and then the fashionable high waisted tummy control that would catch the rolls of her waist. To lift her bust, she would be implanted with silicone prostheses. What did it matter that she was already forbidden by the most recognized doctors in the field if Rosario Altamirano was already determined to take the risk, like so many others...

Daughter, daughter! Something new has just come out for the wrinkles on your face: the laser beam! In several sessions, they will erase the traces of the laughter and pain you have suffered in your life. You will look like a soft canvas, ready to put on makeup, look in the magazines how the makeup is being worn so that you do not stay in the past repeating the one you used in your twenties. Daughter, you are already in your forties, you must use all these resources, and you will see how you surprise them at the meeting.

The need to be beautiful would justify the pain. With liposuction, 50 pounds of fat, the product of good food would be aspirated. But, contrary to what happened in past centuries, when heavy and rosy women were synonymous with beauty, health and well-being, in these new times, the thinner, bulimic and anorexic, without flesh to show or touch, they only showed their bones. Rosario was sure that the remaining rolls would be imprisoned by the 'Feminine Beauty' tummy control and her lips, with the intervention of Dr. Ramiro, would be fleshy and howling with sensuality, while her aquiline nose would finally be upturned, looking for the sky, as if looking up, unlike the parrot nose that tormented her so much. In addition, Dr. Ramiro would also fix her chin so that there would be harmony in her face.

A year passed, witnessing the sweaty nights and loaded with the pain produced by liposuction, the trauma of her crushed nose molded to the surgeon's liking. Days when it was difficult for her to get used to the new chin and the stunning breasts that invited them to be shamelessly exhibited. The Botox wrinkle remover acted like sharp knives that penetrated her skin, she felt in the furrows the burning for those years that had passed in which her skin had already lost the elasticity necessary to look young.

It didn't matter that those furrows had witnessed

previous experiences, if we are now in the 21st century, when independent women are still subject to the image of the models who appear in fashion magazines. What happened to feminists? With the enrichment of the intellect that they proclaimed so much? With the search for an identity of its own? Rosario knew that at the meeting no one would ask her about her career, or her achievements, but that if they saw her as the cover of a magazine, she would surely be the center of attention. How many more interventions would she have to endure to look like a woman of the 21st century?

After all the surgeries, the day of the long-awaited second debut arrived: hairdresser's hairstyle, freshly painted nails and the outfit lying on the bed. A doll made up in pastel tones, Rosario was ready to wear the Yves Saint Lauren suit, the latest fashion. Sweating, she jumped, jumped, and jumped trying to make the body suit fulfill its function. Victoria Secret's bra would lift her breasts, and that fuchsia mouth lipstick would hide the reality of carrying Botox toxin between her lips, or so she thought, because it was enough to see women with Botox to realize that the thickness of the lips was not natural. All those who were summoned were at the meeting, thirty in total. All with Botox, body suits, concealing and shaping bra and liposuction, showing the identity of the fictional woman of the third millennium. What happen with woman in the 21st century? What about being different, creative and capable?

There is Rosario, like the other 29, not knowing who to greet. None of them managed to recognize the others and all of them impeccable, with their anxious souls in front of a broken mirror that did not reflect them,

The Dance of the Shadows

because they only wanted to stand out.

Maria Gabriela Madrid

Hellish Paradise

For Marisela Torres, tasting a ripe banana wrap with the melted cheese sliding down her delicate throat was one of her pleasures comparable to the divine, exclusively coming from the beyond. She also liked fried plantains and mango with salt. Owner of a small seaside resort on the shores of the clear and crystalline blue sea, envied by European tourists, whose beaches stand out for having rocky sand with round and oval rocks that cover their ground, the opposite of these Margarita Island' beaches free of rocks, with white and soft sand to step on. The only similarity to Nice-France were women sunbathing their uncovered breasts, enjoying the soft and hot sun until sunset.

For Esteban, France was paradise on earth and Paris, the city of eternal romance, with its museums, the Champs-Elysées, the Eiffel Tower, the Seine River, the Bridge of Sighs, where so many prisoners led to their deaths left their last breath there. Paris, with its wines, cheeses, bistros and coffee places was the city that stimulated the best of its being. A student of architecture, Esteban was enraptured by the surrounding domes and chapels, by the gargoyles placed as guardians of hundreds of years old buildings. And to think that there were barely a hundred days left until finishing the semester at the university. Enthusiastic about the imminent vacation, he convinced, ticket in hand, his French companions to visit Margarita Island; and very soon, they ended up in Venezuela.

A Caracas native, although he felt he was from Margarita island at heart, Esteban was a lover of cheese patties, shredded meat and dogfish. Margarita island, with its imposing hotels on the edge of the beaches, the gated communities with paradisiacal houses and that duty-free shopping center, was undoubtedly an island like few others: beautiful women, nightlife, casinos and freedom to do and undo. The hotel, with all services included, promised them an unforgettable stay. During the day, the beach; in the afternoon, the Club Med-style theater; and at night, the walk through the city.

On the third day of arrival, Dominique, Claude and Esteban decided to go on adventures. They left the hotel heading for "Beach The Angel." Amazed, they observed the seller of necklaces, rings and bracelets, with his briefcase full of white, pink, large, medium and small pearls that he tried to sell at ridiculous prices to Europeans, because by exchanging euros for bolivars, the advantage was amazing. Blessed are the French with that powerful currency, which left the dollar weaker every day, which was still desired by Latin Americans.

Under the radiant sun, among oils and sunscreens, they were toasted on the sand.

Looking for excitement, Dominique went out to sea. The jet ski, jumping like a dolphin, hit the waves with great force. Claude, passionate about marine life, dived in with his diving equipment. Amazed, he saw eels, urchins, sea horses, multicolored fish, and seaweed of all shades of greenish and brown. Meanwhile, Esteban, tired of sunbathing, wanted to grab something else, some food that would satisfy his pent-up hunger.

Walking along the beach he arrived at the beach attended by Marisela and the snack drove him crazy. After drinking the cocktail of shrimp, clams and oysters with lemon wedges, he began to watch in amazement the delicate figure of Marisela, who, "machete (large knife with wide blade)" in hand, with accurate blows, opened a coconut in half. The delicious water and the whitish, watery skin of the coconut captivated him.

He is attracted to Marisela by her tan, the long black hair, but her inability to speak was what he liked the most. Born mute, the young woman communicated by signs and gestures.

It's perfect, Esteban thought, there will be no arguments, just pure attraction. Without wasting time, Esteban and Marisela set out to share the remaining days. Just two days before flying back, Dominique went to "Beach The Angel" on his jet ski, Claude went snorkeling and Esteban with Marisela went walking on the white sand. Suddenly the sky became heavier and took on a very dark blackish color. Strong winds, lightning and thunder unleashed the storm, or perhaps an unprecedented hurricane. In a matter of seconds, the waves rose immensely, and the tide rose. Closer and closer to the resort, Esteban and Marisela watched it in terror as people ran terrified trying to save their lives. It was not a normal storm; suddenly, a wave about six meters high swept over them, who ran and tried to look for Dominique and Claude. They turned around all the time and, without turning into salt, terrified they witnessed that hell.

Children, women and men disappeared before their eyes. Nervously, they saw the magnitude of the water and the waves that approached mercilessly.

Dominique and his motorbike were sucked into the fury of the ocean, perhaps they were lying at the bottom of the sea. Claude drowned, and perhaps one day he will be thrown onto the beach. Esteban and Marisela, mounted on a roof, listened to the screams as they looked at the corpses thrown by the sea. The water level was rising: shacks, spas, houses and hotels were flooded and swept away by the fury of the sea. The inhabitants of "Beach The Angel" could see how nature took revenge after so many centuries of abuse. The ozone layer, perforated by the emission of gases and pollution, was supposedly the direct cause of climate change.

More hurricanes, more droughts, more floods and now this intense storm has starred great destruction. An inclement wave gave Esteban an accurate blow, leaving him unconscious. The indomitable wave dragged Marisela to suck her in. Now it was the waves, the avid and hungry waves, that in their path swept away what was left on earth.

More than once the seers had communicated their revelations by leaving them in writing and in them, they preached the end of an abused planet: natural disasters, wars everywhere. It was the forgotten nature that was now taking its revenge.

Taste of Blood

Rosa, Rosa the tuberculous! Just as the song says. Although Rosa is sick, it is not from tuberculosis. But she has an emaciated face, bluish skin, pronounced dark circles under her eyes and glands with protrusions in her throat about to burst. Weeks have passed in which Rosa does not get out of bed. They say that her illness is one of love. Her boyfriend Reinaldo went to the United States to try his luck, because the country where he was born does not offer him security or a job that will help him lead a decent life.

Rosa asked Miss Elvira. Try to get up and walk, at least change the environment so that your lungs breathe pure air. Attentive to her advice, Rosa sat up and, with her robe tied around her waist, went down the stairs that led her to the kitchen. Hungry, she opened the fridge and took some "Dulce Real", a Venezuelan dessert, between her fingers. The scrambled eggs wrapped in honey slipped through the cracks of her hands, so by licking her fingers she enjoyed the flavor of the Christmas party ahead of time.

"Daughter, take a warm bath, get ready because the guests are almost here."

The table was dressed in the white linen tablecloth freshly washed by the Portuguese women, those divine angels, connoisseurs of the secrets of laundry. Birds of paradise flowers and green foliage branches adorned the dining room centerpiece. Miss

Elvira oversaw the pork and the tenderloin in plum sauce, while Rosa was in charge of the chicken salad and the almond salad with raisins.

"Daughter, it's great that you are smelling good and already dressed. What perfume are you wearing? Surely it is the jasmine one that the young man gave you. Are you still thinking about him? Look, he's already gone, it's better to forget and get rid of that idea of looking for him. Texas is not your land and, Rosa, life is not easy."

"Oh mom, don't worry, until this virus goes away, I won't go to the United States."

"Go and open the door, the first guests have already arrived."

"Mom: It's Uncle Antonio and Grandma Ernestina."

"Come in, come into the hall. Today we must celebrate that we are still all together."

The unmentionable has all Venezuelans with their hair standing on end. That if you leave and don't come back, that the thugs are on the hunt on every corner. Even Russian vessels are ready to fight. And to think that now the rebels act like lambs in the face of the plans of the unmentionable president.

"Miss Elvira: turn up the volume, that's the "buddy' bagpipes song. The one that calls for a revolution."

And between maracas and drums, those present, elevated, longed for a different future.

"Elvira, Jorge Luis: everything is already arranged for the departure, the war we are living through is not contained and the one that is coming to us is already lost."

"Oh Antonio, I'm not ready. This is my life: My people, my house, my things, nothing is going to happen. Remember that we are not an island."

"Yes, but by thinking like that the unnamed has taken a lot of ground... Well, let's toast he would change his mind before it's too late."

"Well, here's the sangria, refreshing and with chunks of fruit and crushed ice, just the way we like it. Hey, didn't Aunt Luisa say she was coming? Could something has happened to her? Rosa asked with a distressed face."

"Oh Rosa, don't be fatalistic, surely, she changed her mind and is at the Rivero house. We'd better sit down for dinner."

"Pass me the cream punch and plum sauce. This tenderloin is too tasty."

"Thank you, Antonio, Rosa did it."

"Rosa, you have good seasoning, it's exquisite."

Three Kings dinner, whiskey, wine, cream punch and refreshing cocktails.

"Hurry to the garden, the Villanueva are going to start the show."

Hours in which the sky is dressed in colors and lights. Fireworks. Boom, bang, boom, cannon shots of nostalgia and celebration bid farewell to the old year and welcome the new one full of old unfulfilled promises.

Christmas without baby Jesus, there are no more children hanging around the house, only adults exchanging dreams.

"Rosa: When do you have the appointment at the embassy?"

"Tomorrow. And I will bring more than they ask for. This time they can't deny it to me. It will be my third attempt."

"Well, hopefully you'll be lucky. I did the same and even took the airplane ticket, but they left me hanging. They say that since the expulsion of the ambassador they do not give visas."

"I don't think so uncle, anyone would say that after such an outrage they would close the embassy and look they haven't. The truth is that it is like a game. Insults come and go, but for me that if they continue to send the gringos the crude oil, our commander in chief will continue to be in power."

"Rosa, are you fatalistic again?"

"Elvira, let her speak."

"Who wants coffee?" Elvira asked.

Everyone immediately signed up to drink caffeine. The one that wakes up the dead with so many names, blacky, brown, "guayoyo" (watery coffee), coffee with milk, etc., etc., etc."

"There is no milk."

"Sister, are you kidding me?"

"Antonio, you can't get it anywhere."

"I think they are the damn hoarders. The new rumor is that next year there will be no meat or eggs."

"Oh woman, what a calamity, come and let's dance this merengue! Leave the coffee brewing for later."

Bagpipes songs, salsa, merengues, cumbias and drums incite those present to move their waists and feet until they burst. Diverse rhythms were played until dawn.

"Rosa: I think they're ringing the doorbell."

"Oh yes, it must be Aunt Luisa."

At that moment she opens the door and gives way to the young man from darkness. Gun in hand and with a voice still like a child, he shouts at the top of his lungs to everybody to get on the ground.

Whining, screams and pleas disturb the thug who, moving around the gun, promises that no one will be killed.

"Where's the food?"

"Go upstairs, the dining room is upstairs," said Miss Elvira.

"And what do you think of me, I am not stupid, I won't move from here, go and do nothing or I'll break you all."

"What's going on here? They left the door open."

"Shut up, Aunt Luisa, and get on the ground, Rosa ordered."

"Oh, but why?"

Turning his face, the thug, still with his hands smeared with plum sauce, points at Aunt Luisa and, believing that she is going to attack him, shot her.

"Since I killed her, now, I'll have to kill you all so that there won't be any witnesses."

Whining that were silenced one by one. Restless bodies.

The neighbors heard the shooting, and believed it was fireworks.

A country of contrasts, where the inhabitants risk their lives every day, and hope at the end of the day to have coffee, to smell the damp earth of the country where they were born.

The Dance of the Shadows

On New Year's Eve, where in the middle of the party, thugs win points in the all-out war.

Solutions

All the people I spoke to fell short of the changes that had taken place in the city where I was born. Rivers of cars passed by and even parked for hours at the famous traffic jams of the highways. People who commune daily with the strident sounds produced by the radios at full volume.

"But hey, pal, turn it down! Your pot (referring to his car) is going to burst."

Three in the afternoon and Daniel couldn't wait to get to his parents' house. It was long hours of flight, the inopportune lady who didn't stop talking, the child who screamed with the lungs of the best opera singer. High-pitched screams that penetrated for nine hours in the hidden corners of his brain, and, in mid-flight, having to listen to the whistles of the baseball fan every time the plane fell into turbulence. It was a hellish flight that anticipated what was to come.

"Son, but how badly the Anglo-Saxons have treated you. You're fatter and even balder, and what happened to your skin? It was very white and now looks tanned, just like the construction workers."

"Mom, I'm going to rest, there are few days, and we have to coordinate the burial of the old man and the sale of the house."

"Go away, I'll wake you up for dinner later."

Finally, lying in the hammock, he began to dream. Reminiscences unveiled during restful sleep.

Daniel did not want to wake up because he had an athletic body and more than four hairs floating while driving at high speed. Paradise where the policeman ignored those who broke the law with bribes, but now with all the set-up police controls on the streets, those who did not have the required license to circulate were fined with high sums of money.

"What happens my friend?"

"I promise I'll apply for my license tomorrow," he says, placing the Ray-Ban glasses on the seat and taking out a few bills from his pocket to bribe.

"Look, man, this time I'll let you go, but give me more, I have five little boys to feed."

Waking up sweaty at such a request, he breathed when he saw that it was only a dream.

"Daniel: Dinner is served. Look, I prepared what you like the most."

Different trays. There was fried ripe plantain, shredded meat, black beans, and rice with a fried egg on top to complete the dish called "Pabellon."

"Thank you, mom, it looks very good," at the same time of leaning over to help himself.

"Mijo, eat a little" and taking away his spoon she served him three grains of rice, half a banana, three rows of shredded meat and a quarter of the fried egg. "That's it, this is more than enough!"

"Son, you can't imagine how expensive everything is. You can no longer go to supermarkets; they always charge triple. Tomorrow, we will go to the market, and you will see how the money will last."

"You must come and carry the bags, okay?"

140

"All right, he answered," pretending to chew what little he had in his mouth to deceive the crackles in his insides that betrayed his hunger. Reviewing the papers, he was surprised by the costs of funeral homes, the land that was never purchased, and even the cost of soup and snacks for mourners.

It took several days to get used to the new currency, and he realized how the budget had skyrocketed.

"Son, come, you haven't seen your father yet. There he is in his room, as if he was asleep."

As he entered, he stopped at the threshold of the door. Seeing him motionless, without the vitality that characterized him, made him understand how ephemeral it is to be alive.

"Mom: Have you called them yet? They must come and give you the death certificate and pick him up."

"Yes, Mijo, but everything is so expensive that I thought I'd save that little money for my old age. Here's the freezer that we used when your dad brought the shrimp and fish sacks from the coast."

Stunned, Daniel put his hands to his temples, making useless calculations because the next day inflation would turn prices higher. Waking up to birdsong was part of the charm of living east of the city. But because of the urgency of that morning, he heard screams:

"Hurry up, son, you have to go to the bank to withdraw the cash."

"But hey, Mom, can't we pay by credit card there?"

"No, Mijo, but don't worry, I know what I'm doing."

"Is that place different from supermarkets?"

"Just a little, you'll see."

Hearing her number, Rosa ran with her ticket in hand and said: "Give me thirty thousand bolivars in singles bills."

"I guess you meant three hundred thousand" asked Daniel.

"Yes, but now we must remove the zeros."

"But mom, that way it can't last."

Let's go to the market. Just get used to the fact that you must remove the zeros from everything," she replied, laughing mischievously at the face of such a dark situation.

"Hey, lady, you are not going to have much money. Since they opened the market, every Tuesday we must take singles bills out of the vault and they even ask us to give hundreds of thousands in exchange," he explained, laughing out loud while he gave her the ten bolivares bills.

"Walk, Mijo," she said, without saying goodbye to the cashier because of the haste to get to the market before twelve.

The parking lot now was full of good quality fruit, vegetables, cheese and other products. The faces disgruntled of unfriendly people started to run and like an stampede went side by side to get the food.

"Mijo run, there are not going to be any cassava left!

And Daniel, slow, not understanding yet what was happening, felt a push in his butt up.

"You must run here."

Daniel, with his jeans tied to his waist, felt how when he ran his "Michelin" rolls jumped. The white linen "guayabera" highlighted his fat arms, ready to load the purchased goods.

"Mom, I can't take it anymore."

"No son, we still need to grab milk and cheese."

"Bags, bags, who wants more bags!" Take advantage of the fact that the pound is at three!"

And Daniel understood at the top of his lungs that in supermarkets you can get certain vegetables and fruits at less than three per pound, so shouting from the top of his lungs, he said: "Bags? Why bags? If the biggest bag is me."

As tired as a donkey he feels the burning of the cuts made by the weight he was carrying.

At that moment Rosa puts the purchased goods away in the pantry and continues to the freezer.

A full moon night where Daniel, with his glass of crushed ice and whiskey drinks slowly, looking for solutions.

On the terrace, surrounded by "Chaguaramos" and palm trees, he glimpses black smoke in the distance, the product of those who have died. At that moment he decides to put the house up for sale, the moment he goes up to the old man's room and loads him into the freezer. Grill ready to be used in the wee hours of the morning. In the dark night, he will cut his father into pieces to roast him and reduce him to ashes.

Money saved for mom's old age.

Plane that leaves without Daniel. A country of madmen where the clever ones have anecdotes to tell.

The Open Wound

Sometimes reality surpasses fiction and this is what has happened in a country where the Andean mountains give the air of mystery of the territory not yet conquered. Beaches where the water is so clear that you can see your own feet in the depth. Sand hills, oil fields, natural resources and a climate that is sunny or rainy during the year. Letting its beauty aside, this country has an open wound. A wound that today bleeds profusely like the strong current of the Orinoco River. Every time I visit my country, I see how it deteriorates more and more. As a sign of desperation, I sit down and press my temples with my hands. I need to get an explanation for all the deception that surrounds the former President of Venezuela. So, I grabbed a pen and paper and started writing once again about the injustices that happen in my country. The former President or rather Dictator of Venezuela was a man of great Spanish oratory and his many facets motivated writers, psychologists and others to write about him. For fourteen years he used the media to manipulate information and reinvent himself with the goal of perpetuating himself in power. Years ago, a film based on Socialism of the 21st Century was on the billboard. The film showed him as a revolutionary man who wanted the best for his people.

Unfortunately, his policies did the opposite and as the film was made in a controlled environment, this turned out to be just another propaganda for the regime.

To date, only a few have food on the table and clothing, but that can change at any time. Most people live outside the ghettos. These people have felt in their stomachs the intense pain of having nothing to eat, or nowhere to go when they are sick or injured. At first, the majority supported him. Many were attracted by his power of persuasion and believed that change was near. Hopefully, many hoped there would be social justice. Those were years in which money was not a problem because oil was being quoted at high prices. As a result, floods of money poured into the country, and hopeful people believed it would be used to improve under-resourced hospitals, build housing, create new jobs, provide educational materials, and pay back wages. But instead, suitcases full of money were sent to other countries. The money was used to fund projects and manipulate the results of presidential elections in other countries, while in Venezuela, due to voracious inflation, people could not pay rent, buy medicines, or have access to electricity and water from the street. Even though the government has had the highest amounts of money coming into its coffers, it is embarrassing to see how it has built fewer homes than previous governments. Now it is common to see supermarkets with empty shelves: for months you can't get meat, or milk, or cheese, or rice, or toilet paper... The same is happening with medicines. Patients who depend on them can die if they do not take them in due time.

Tired and with my eyes full of tears, I put the pen on the table. Not long ago, my father, a victim of emphysema, almost died because he couldn't take his medicines. For a week his treatment was suspended until the necessary medicines arrived from another country at the door of the house. Tired and hungry, I heard the rumbling of my stomach asking for food. I opened the refrigerator, took out some lentils and heated them. This time I would eat them without rice (due to the shortage).

The anticipation of eating them made my salivary glands activate, and I knew they wouldn't be as tasty as eating them with rice. As soon as I finished eating, I picked up the pen and started writing again. What happened to all of us having a better future? All the evidence points to the fact that it has all been a vulgar lie and for those who still believe in their Socialism 21st Century, as soon as they realize that they have been manipulated, the disillusionment will be devastating and will cause more revolts.

At first people were surprised to see how Chavez instigated hatred and division among Venezuelans, resulting in housing developments and streets not being able to be transit by the opposition. Also, at the beginning of his term, the government set up outpatient clinics to assist the poor, but now a few have been abandoned and closed. It seems that the lifestyle of Venezuelans has not improved, but, on the contrary, it has most people suffering. The middle class is disappearing and, contrary to false statistics, the current government has increased poverty.

Consumer power has decreased, and many are unable to cover their basic needs. A few years ago, changes in economic policies made people poorer. The offices of the stock market were closed, and Venezuela became a country where criminals run free. Some time ago, videos appeared where people affiliated with the government appeared killing innocent people. Within a week of being seen in the video, they were already free on the street. They were not prosecuted. The government, like an octopus, took over the judicial system and other institutions with its tentacles. It all began fourteen years ago, and Venezuela changed to be a country whose central government brought together all the power to control the existence of its citizens.

The Armed Forces acquired weapons with the purpose of oppressing anyone who protests. Now the wound in Venezuela is deeper and the intimidation of citizens under fear and force occurs daily. Innocent people have been killed. They were people who sought to be heard. They were students, mothers and fathers protesting in peaceful demonstrations. Not long ago the government took control of the oil company (PDVSA) and laid off thousands of workers capable of doing their job.

Many protested and the marches reached more than two million people on the streets, entire highways were the scene of people shouting and demanding justice and freedom of expression. The high-pitched and sometimes low-pitched sound of spoons banging pots and pans became the symbol of government opponents.

Many radio and television stations were forced to close their doors and the only channel that broadcast freely was bought by the government and its directive was changed.

Recreational properties and businesses were expropriated from their rightful owners by the simple wish of the former dictator. The list of unemployed grew every day. The private sector hit by the government saw how foreign investors did not want to invest in the country. Time and time again, human rights and laws were violated, and we even saw Cuban personnel working at immigration posts, violating Venezuelan' sovereignty. Bribing was part of the routine at the international airport every time a passenger tried to leave the country. The crime unleashed and the return of the kidnapping industry, like a terminal cancer, spread throughout the country.

Suddenly I noticed that it was getting dark, I hid what I had written and went to the street with a pot and spoon in hand ready to make it sound during the march.

For hours I walked along the highway. The purpose was to go downtown. It is a dangerous area because it belongs to those who support the government. Near downtown we ran into the National Guard. Liquid gas was expelled against us, and many were beaten and arrested.

It was a peaceful demonstration where people unexpectedly hid behind trees, buildings and bushes as they started shooting at us. Many resulted in fatalities. That night I returned home emotionally stunned. I took some pills to calm the anxiety and tried to write again when my father told me about the sale of Orinoco.

With contempt I shouted: "Is he going to sell more land?"

It was all a farce. All the insults going back and forth between the two governments did not prevent business from continuing. The USA embassy never closed and now I know that it had all been a lie. Investors also wanted a piece of the pie. The Orinoco is ours and it must remain so. Has the damage done to the nation not been enough? What happens now with Chavez's Socialism 21st Century? What about improving the standard of living of Venezuelans? Will Maduro fight the kidnapping industry? Or is it perhaps another of the tentacles to keep people afraid? Has it not been enough to hijack our freedoms and standard of living? will I be able to put my life at risk of being kidnapped again? Can my desire to see family and friends be enough to put my fears aside? Who knows? But at least I know that nothing can replace the sweet aroma of the wet earth, the bite of the arepa at three o clock in the morning, and the soothing sound of crickets in the night. Nothing lasts forever and the chains that oppress us today will sooner or later be removed, and Venezuelans will regain the freedom that was kidnapped 14 years ago.

(Update: The dictatorship has been in power since 1998; 27 years ago, and counting...)

Mamoon

Maria Cristina's life was always marked by strange circumstances. Before birth, her mother, Claudia, agonized with pain. Only insults came out of her mouth, screams that cried out not to give birth, until she finally was operated on. The cesarean section and anesthesia promised a calm, routine delivery. Ernesto, strong, corpulent, with a dark complexion, was in charge of administering the anesthesia: a cocktail of halothane gas, muscle relaxants and oxygen, so much of this, so much of that would lead her to a deep sleep to wake up hours after the event. As soon as the surgery began, Claudia's inert and unconscious body convulsed relentlessly as the screams continued. The wear and tear of those in the room and herself were already unsustainable. They couldn't understand how she could speak if she was asleep. Claudia's full rejection of little Maria Cristina, a girl barely hours old, whom her mother already saw as the great hindrance of her life, was already decreed: her dreams of independence would be tied to the existence of this new being. Years passed, and with an inadequate upbringing, Maria Cristina never experienced the tacit complicity that should have existed between mother and daughter and that she would always seek. But now, at 20 years old, the risk and adrenaline at its peak was what motivated her to continue living. That afternoon she was determined. She longed to follow other paths, not the one pointed out by a castrating mother, always reminding her

Maria Gabriela Madrid

of what she has sacrificed because she had given her life. After packing a few changes of clothes, Maria Cristina headed for the small white and sky-blue airport where only three planes were in line to depart.

In that town of dusty streets, you could see the sawmills destroying the flora and fauna. They never planted new trees for each tree cut down while the belief that natural resources never run out on the contrary to what was reported in First World countries. And to think that it was their own corporations, although in Third World territory, that cut down the trees incessantly.

Maria Cristina went to a lawless war that had been imagined and planned years before the invasion. The maximum leader had fabricated the causes of invading a country crushed by a tyrant, but at the same time tired of previous invasions that, like this one, threatened their way of life. Now it would be his Arabic food mixed with Mac Donalds and Burger King; their music, in competition with the acid rock of Kiss, Pink Floyd, the Rolling Stones, an invasion that came to stay. With such concerns in her mind, Maria Cristina left, leaving that town that suffocated her, leaving her Central American country that had made a pact with the invaders to send soldiers, fresh bait for export. The arduous training took her six months in the capital city. She knew the basics, like shooting. Its arrival to Iraq was not very welcoming, other groups already pre-established did not give her a chance. Her cinnamon skin caused a rejection other than those of her mother could have had. The arid months of battle sensitized her to the horror of seeing innocent children mutilated, dead, scattered in the streets after each attack. An earthly hell were several soldiers preferred suicide to continue in such an unjustified war, where smart bombs, which were nothing of the sort, because there were more failed targets and it was already customary to hear: "It fell on a hospice! It fell on a wedding celebration!" while blood flowed, and destruction was total.

Day by day and month by month, Maria Cristina won the appreciation of her battalion colleagues despite her almost exclusively gestural communication, or in deficient English, a poor vocabulary that during the conflict could be fatal.

One afternoon in March, some of her companions, blinded by sandstorms, making gestures like grimaces and uttering screams that could not be read, were shot down and she was trapped in the hands of Mamoon, a tall, strong, black-haired man, surrounded by the sand, who, imposing his authority, hid her in a cave.

Tied up, Maria Cristina fought day and night trying to untie herself. She felt that she would die, while Mamoon, in the solitude that surrounded him, visited her frequently. The hatred generated by feeling like her prisoner and the recollection of the first rape was an indelible memory that tore her soul out.

She hated the rubbing of that skin, its smell, the unwanted proximity, although, with the passage of time, the rapes no longer seemed so painful to her. Aware that this was her destiny, she was adapting more and more to what awaited her to live. After six months, Mamoon let go of her, only to find that she was now the one who didn't want to leave him. Could it be the Stockholm Syndrome that affects the kidnapped? Just as it happened to Patty Hearst, daughter of a prominent American family, dominated, in love, controlled by her kidnappers, to the point of having participated in a bank robbery!

Maria Cristina would never have imagined that this rapist had become an essential part of her broken being. A Catholic by upbringing, at first, she saw how her prayers vanished, but now she didn't even pray anymore...

Married under a tent in the desert, they tasted chickpeas with tahini, fermented milk, kibbeh, and tabbouleh, food that was new to her, who had just tasted the kibbeh with lentils, that rice and potato balls filled with mince and seasoned with butter and wheat (a variant of her Creole lentils with rice.) In the simple ceremony, only the gold was missing, usually a gift from the groom, which would represent his love for her. As tradition dictated, the bride wore necklaces, rings and other costume jewelry.

At a traditional wedding, Arabic music, with its fast pace, would have reminded Maria Cristina of her country of origin, but the only music she heard was the shootings coming closer.

Missing were the dances in which the women dance among themselves, with contortions and sinuous movements, and the men's dancing in circle. Men and women rarely dance in pairs. The Arab matrons, less modernized than men, do not even allow themselves to be greeted, they run out to avoid any contact.

It had become late, and as night fell, the threat of a final contest grew. The shots could be heard closer and closer, but she, in that distant country and without a common language to express herself, had already begun to feel the rejection of those around her and her spirit, tired of fighting to be accepted, had run out of energy, without desire to continue fighting, without a desire to challenge and at that moment she understood that Mamoon could never make her happy. Her mother and her people had been left behind and she knew that now only death itself could free her from a war that will have no end.

(Update: The Iraq war ended in 2011)

Peace Corps

Leticia lost her daughter and was plunged into great loneliness, only the endless walks among unknown beings gave her the energy required to help the dispossessed. As an antidote to tedium, she offered to volunteer to go to the country where the four winds intersect, dry land plateaus, sparse vegetation and flaccid cows with crows flying over their heads, anticipating the process of decomposition.

Villages eradicated by horsemen, who supported by the government leave behind the last breath of those who were once fortunate enough to live. Land of drums, a region of oblivion, where the hooves of horses raise the dust mixed with the blood of the fallen and those who survive are humiliated day and night, slowly drying the spirit of their victims.

Leticia cooks in one of the camps belonging to the peacekeepers. This space is occupied by tents that leave little space for recreation.

"Leticia, here is Adede, she is strong, she can help you and, in her eyes, there is still peace."

"So, what, shouldn't I be with the other children?"

"Yes, but it can help you and give you back what you lost."

Annoyed by the imposition, Leticia threw away the wooden ladle and sent Adede to stir the saucepan.

It's lunchtime and entire lines of people are waiting for the day's portion.

Tired at her young age, once the kitchen was tidied up, Adede took in her hands the photo of her mother, the only memory of whom lovingly caressed her curly hair and promised her that soon everything would get better.

Hollow nights in which silence is the companion of lonely souls. For Leticia, having kicked her daughter out of the house was not so much because she wanted to go to war, but because she had fallen in love with a damn horseman.

Now under the same sky, she knew she would never see her among those who inhabit the camp.

Months passed, and the dwindling aid was evidence of the international community's deaf ears. The deaths were not only the product of violence, but also of malnutrition.

Every morning, Adede's arrival in the kitchen flooded those in the room with joy. Rowdy, she sang while she was doing her chores, but that day there was something else reflected in her face, it was the purity of her gaze when she sensed that she would soon recover the lost affection.

As there was not enough wood to cook, Leticia was one of those sent to pick it up but using the excuse of migraine she hid her fear from the horsemen and ordered Adede to go in her place. Go, hurry, for only a mile away are the bushes waiting to be cut down.

Late in the afternoon, Leticia went to rest in the tent, when suddenly, next to the pillow, she saw the photo of her daughter, Adede's mother. Desperate, it took her several minutes to understand and without stopping screaming she anticipated what was going to happen. Without thinking, she ran to catch up with them. The deafening noise of the hooves lifting the earth were the sign that she was too late. The horsemen had already departed, and scarcely half a mile from the camp were the warm, lifeless bodies of the outraged young women. Crying inconsolably and with gasping breath, she turned their faces one by one trying to fix them in her memory. In Adede's absence, Leticia felt relief that she had not been killed but also pain because she feared that once she was raped, she would be the sex slave of the horsemen.

Suddenly, the wind picked up against the bushes and tearing off part of their foliage revealed the dark face and curly hair of Adede, who squatted, hugged her knees, swaying without noticing Leticia's presence.

Dimegüeyes, Saviors of the Human Race

The global climate changed a long time ago and places where the temperature was hot were now showing frigid temperatures. Even though the walls of my apartment were cold I wanted to leave the windows open. I was sitting reading the latest news when I felt my body temperature rise. It was already disheartening to see entire communities disappear, and even harder to see countries in constant attack, but now I needed to be focused to be able to translate the newfound information. It was the only way in which the "Dimegüeyes" and the public would continue to be deceived regarding the events of the moment.

My great dream as a military journalist was always to be in the middle of the action and not behind a desk, but the "Center of Universal Journalism" wanted to keep me close. My ability to speak "Dimegüeyes" and other languages made me a treasure in the current situation.

I was working for many years with the military, and it was known that in war you had to manipulate the truth.

I admit that I miss the years when the public lived a normal life and would have wished that people would protest the use of machines in daily life instead of having remained silent.

Maria Gabriela Madrid

Those were the years when machines did the work of humans. These were the years in which the military centers changed the way of recruiting future soldiers.

The navy for a while used the old tactics of going to supermarkets and universities, but at the same time they also created centers full of computers and war games.

Military personnel allowed anyone to play and then had them register for missions where their lives would never be at risk: seated soldiers, from any center, sent drones that launched missiles at other countries. It was fabulous because since there was no person inside the drone, the casualties were always enemies.

Faster than anyone could anticipate, machines ended up doing the work of humans. I still remember my mother's naivety laughing at new technology. She never understood the repercussions of the computer doing the cashier's job until she was fired. Then, I had heard that other schools had a toilet cleaner, and a floor-cleaner and since her school was located in a privileged area it finally happened.

"Lupita, don't worry, you know me, and worse things have happened to me. You'll see how I will get a job."

I was ten years old, and I remember Mom coming home smelling like bleach, her face tired and the uncertainty to see me doing my homework. Many times, I read words aloud that Mom did not understand, and yet she just wanted me to learn and live a better life. Study, mijita, study, that is why I work. As she always told me.

She was right: I studied, I went to university and despite having a better situation than many people, the world is no longer what it was.

Now in the year 2060, not only do machines do our jobs, but also countless hidden eyes watch our movements. Surveillance cameras are very sophisticated, they are no longer seen, but they record everything that happens.

2060 is the year when humans are at the bottom of the pyramid: Women's salaries are the same as they were in the golden age, always lower than men's salaries (seventy-seven cents for every dollar earned). Men and some women no longer hold any leadership positions, they are now under the control of robots supervised by Special Forces.

The soldiers of the navy are not human, but a hybrid of human beings, animals and machinery. Scientists, after the advances in genetic intervention, manipulated human DNA with the DNA of other animals and created soldiers capable of running at the speed of the panther, having the vision of squid, the hearing of bats, the strength of gorillas, and the intelligence of humans.

Robots were originally only going to be used in war, but now they were everywhere. Humans and the "Dimegüeyes" are marginalized to the point of living in the most extreme poverty. Many men and women are in hiding, but those who could not escape are in hospitals, waiting for their organs to be removed.

Since the origin of humanity, women have been an essential part of reproduction, but now scientists are trying to create a super organ that allows robots to multiply themselves. The news is devastating and means that humans will no longer be needed, and only in a few months, robots will be indestructible.

Here I am, trembling, and I can't keep reading the news on the wall that serves as a screen. I am so engrossed that my gaze only shows emptiness. My job is to tell the public lies so that the Special Forces will prevent any rebellion. Instead of translating the news, I grabbed my coat and looked at the sensor that opens the door to my apartment. Then I went downstairs and looked at the sensor that opens the door to my building. It would have been great to be able to sneak away, but the implant in my ear reminds me that with the satellite system, the Special Forces know my every move.

"Lupita, here, here."

"Yes, I saw you."

"Lorena, we have only few months. You must summon everyone."

"What happened?"

"Scientists are close to creating a super organ that will allow robots to reproduce. Do you see? Humans are not going to be necessary. Tell them that we must fight and, Lorena, this time I'm not going to lie to the public anymore. Now I understand what my mother always told me: a woman's ability to make decisions is a right that must be fought for and defended. It's our right. It is our right to choose what kind of life we want to have and how we want to achieve it. Lorena, promise me that you will raise your voice against injustices, sex trafficking, and violence. Promise me that you will fight for the fair treatment of women and men."

"Oh Lupita, you're getting sentimental. Besides, you know that at least I'm going to try. Have you heard that most countries are surrendering to Special Forces?"

"Yes, and the reason is because the Special Forces know the language and know their plans in advance; but in our case, although we are few, our advantage is that they have no idea of the language of the "Dimegüeyes," that is why they have always wanted me to continue translating for them, but I am not going to allow it anymore."

"But Lupita, if you don't, you know what can happen to you."

Lupita, with moist eyes and a triumphant smile, drew with the tip of her index finger a large screen in the sky and wrote: "People, the time to fight has come."

"Is it the implant in your brain that allows you to do that, or is it the implant in your ear?"

"Lorena, the implant in my ear informs the special forces of my location and the implant in my brain transforms my thoughts into actions. Do you remember when "Six Senses Technology" came out?"

"How do you think I can forget such a day. It was so amazing and revolutionary to see how people could draw a phone in the palm of their hand and be able to make a phone call or also draw a circle on their wrist and be able to see the time."

"Yes, I remember that technology came out in the golden age, but for most people it was too much to deal with. Well, the truth is that to use that technology it was necessary to have an implant in the brain."

"It is very sad because, like your implant in your ear, special forces can get you at any moment."

"It is ok. I don't care anymore, and I'd rather die fighting with you than continue to lead the life of a traitor."

Suddenly, a Special Forces soldier at the speed of a panther grabbed Lupita and disappeared behind the electrical towers. Instead of being terrified, Lupita thought of the "Dimegüeyes."

She knew that they would fight the Special Forces and that every town and city was on the alert. She also knew that months of torture awaited her because she had been caught and that her body would sooner or later succumb, but never her ideas of equality and freedom. Those ideas that will always prevail with the "Dimegüeyes."

Pamphlets

"Elvia, what are these many pamphlets? What are you up to? Do you think that with this they are going to pay attention to you?"

"Oh, Alberto, at least read it before giving your opinion, please read it out loud."

"For what?"

"Do it, go on. Alberto."

Alberto, adjusting his glasses, began to read out loud: "We live in the age of technology, and we are still in a world of inequalities, where day by day entire populations lack the basic rights to survive: food, housing, education and health. Essential elements to break the cycle of poverty where the creation and implementation of social programs is not enough, but the urgency that the conscience of the collective ceases to be indifferent and works to establish a better future. If you are interested in helping, please contact Elvia de Ponciel at 233-4529."

"Yes Elvia, it sounds good, but this is a waste of time. You are very dreamy. No one is going to call you. Notice that it has been already five years, since the company transferred us, trying to get the engineers or their wives to listen to you and nothing…"

"How are you going to say that; there have been times when they do pay attention to me. Also, with so many unassisted people working around, you must try to do something."

Elvia, knowing the dangers that Wilmer and Pluto faced in the mine, felt that with the pamphlets she could sensitize people to help the dispossessed.

The mine, located on top of a mountain in Ecuador, was the center of largest gold exports. Hundreds of children like Wilmer and Pluto dug out the rock walls with picks and shovels and searched for the coveted mineral in the surrounding mud. For Wilmer and Pluto, it was the ninth time they had gone to the mine, without masks to protect them from the gases. They hoped to secretly take out a gram of gold to sell to usurers for ridiculous prices; gold that would later be resold for more money to jewelers.

Evening was falling, Wilmer and Pluto suffocated and tired were crestfallen at the reality of not having gold to sell, they felt that in order not to faint they had to get some food. Their fragile bodies showed the ravages of malnutrition: Bulging stomachs, dry skin, ulcers and, among others, bones in constant struggle to come out of the skin. Hunger was present, the rumbling and contortions of their stomachs, impossible to calm when they set out walking for twenty minutes towards the inn of Alberto and Elvia de Ponciel, Spaniards living for five years in the mountains.

Wilmer and Pluto, with languid and pleading eyes, entered the restaurant and rushed into the kitchen. Alberto, circular and robust, greeted them all sweaty, but Wilmer, hallucinating, saw him greasy and appetizing, like freshly baked chicken. Enough is enough, Wilmer! Think about how to convince him to give us something to eat, thought Wilmer, trying to get the intrusive voices in his brain to leave him alone.

It's all right, it's all right! he talked to himself in murmurs, while Pluto noticed that Wilmer was elevated, gone in thought, so pulling his shirt brought him out of the trance.

"What's wrong with you, Wilmer? Aren't you going to tell him?"

"Mr. Alberto, we will do whatever you want for a little meal. We haven't eaten for several days!"

"It's okay, it's okay! Wash the dishes and come, there is pork and potatoes for the two of you."

And now it was Alberto who, elevated, his conscience demanded of him: "you've already eaten big guy, beware with having low sugar, diabetic coma, don't you see how round you are,? he wondered, remembering at the same time, while rubbing his belly, that he had to turn off the oven, place the roasted pork on the tray without the red apple now inside his mouth. The potato salad with mayonnaise and capers and the prune sauce were already on the table waiting for Wilmer and Pluto."

"Hurry up shouted Alberto at them, dinner is going to get cold! Go to the table at the back, try not to let the other customers see you. They may feel uncomfortable in your presence in those dirty, torn clothes. At least today the restaurant is not so full."

Wilmer and Pluto didn't stop to even breathe and eat wildly, their small hands dripping with the plum sauce, while they dug their fangs into the pig's feet. A scene so different from the usual one in which in the garbage dump, accustomed to the penetrating stench emitted by rotting food, they compete with men, women, children, rats and dogs while the vultures fly over their heads for the same prey. Alberto, anxious, ate for the third time. For him, the food reminded him of his land. Having worked away from his country for so many years, the time was finally approaching to return to his beloved Spain.

"What are you doing Alberto? Eating again?"

"Oh Elvia, don't bother me and at least since you just arrived say hello to the kids."

"Hello kids."

"That's not right Alberto, you are harming your health, and we could give that food to those in need."

"And you, are you still with that?"

"Really, Alberto, not having so much temptation at hand would help control you, and creating a soup kitchen would help so many hungry people who walk around the region. What do you think?"

"That is not my responsibility. What do you prefer? That we continue to throw away unsold food"

"We can do something good and great, Alberto."

"Look Elvia, I've broken my back working in this restaurant and soon we'll be back in Spain. Today Emilio told me that the company is going to move us in three months. Why that face, woman? Rejoice, or isn't that what you wanted?"

"No Alberto, not anymore, seeing those people unassisted, dying of hunger, I could not abandon them."

"But woman!"

"Yes, and today I was told that I already have the authorization to build the school. I don't ask you much Alberto, just support me."

"Man, are we going to have a school for ourselves? Pluto asked with his eyes bulging. And notebook and pencil?"

"Yes, Pluto, and when school is ready, you're going to have to tell your co-workers from the mine to come, just like anyone who wants to learn to read and write."

"Yes, mam, as you command."

"Elvia, go and serve the customers. They might start saying that we hang out with these ragged kids."

"You children, go away, it's about to get dark."

"Why don't you let them sleep here? There is space in the shed, and this week the shipment of legumes was not so large. This way they will rest in a dry place and will not be alone under the bridge. Look, Wilmer can't handle that cough anymore."

"Well, well," Alberto answered. And Elvia planted a wet kiss on his cheek in gratitude.

The night in the shed allowed Wilmer and Pluto to sleep without being on the defensive. The nights they had to spend under the bridge could not rest completely because they had to stay alert to the homeless and the police of the region.

Back in the mine, Wilmer and Pluto couldn't take it anymore, tiredness, the blisters on their arms and the burns from indiscriminate exposure to the sun were the result of the endless days of work. Two weeks had passed when rumors began to circulate that they would close the mine for not complying with the laws of the government and Wilmer and Pluto, terrified, did not want to imagine how they would earn their daily bread.

The next mine was hours away and they didn't even have money for the bus ticket. With great concern they continued digging with pick and shovel when suddenly there was a detachment of the rocks that would probably leave those who were working that afternoon buried. News quickly reached the media and in a few hours the journalists were with their cameramen speculating about the life and death of the miners.

Alberto, in front of the television, was anxiously awaiting Elvia's arrival. When he saw her, he knew that she had already been given the news. Elvia, eyes swollen from crying so much, refused to believe that Wilmer and Pluto were among the many dead.

"Elvia, I know it's going to be hard for you to accept what happened but face it and let's move forward with our plans. It's been five years with the company and now the possibility of being transferred to Spain is something I don't want to lose."

"Please, Alberto, not now. Listen, they are going to give the latest news about the search."

The search has come to an end and with the approval of the rescue team we announce that there are no survivors.

"Elvia, Elvia, calm down now!"

"And what about the little school?"

"No, they are no longer with us, there are only unknown beings for whom I will not give up the dream of returning."

"Oh Alberto, you don't see the poverty they are in, they have no food, no housing, no one to help them. I can't turn my back on them. You don't understand that we all must collaborate."

"Oh, Elvia and you continue with creating a social conscience. Look: I'm tired of this, if you want us to stay together, what I say will be done. Tomorrow I will let Emilio know that we are willing to continue with the company. Stop crying and start organizing the move."

Children, young people and adults with an uncertain future who will go to work tomorrow for the dream of a gram of gold in the nearest mine. Forgotten beings who are under the hot sun and still hold the hope of receiving help. Alberto has left, leaving Elvia in charge of the restaurant and surrounded by hundreds of pamphlets on the table in constant repetition: "And you, what are you doing for the less fortunate?"

Why?

Christmas has always been a busy time for my family and during December 1976 it not only meant unfurling the nativity scene under the fireplace, the Christmas tree with its decorations under the stairs, placing the Christmas tableware on the table, but also preparing the Christmas dishes. On the night of December 21, the doorbell rang several times, but I decided not to open the door because I knew that one of the Christmas traditions was to ring the doorbell and hide.

That night, after my mom welcomed my aunts and grandmother, her first question was if anyone brought sugar. After everyone nodded their heads, in the blink of an eye, they were all around the table preparing traditional dishes such as "Hallacas," (similar but different than tamale), Ham Bread (Pan de Jamon), Candied Papaya (Dulce de Lechoza) and among many other delicious dishes my favorite dessert called "Dulce Real" (Royal Sweet.)The rhythm of the bagpipes' songs encouraged everyone to dance, but not me, who shyly, knew that it was not appropriate to dance protest songs.

My father once told me that the songs were written to let others know that there were people in Venezuela with nothing to eat, wear, or gift to exchange at Christmastime. Since 1974, Venezuela has become a very rich country. It was the year in which the President of Venezuela nationalized oil and mines and like many other countries. It was believed that it would only be a matter of time before all the inhabitants of the country improved their lifestyle.

Unfortunately, two years later, for most Venezuelans there was not enough food to put on the table. My family was well off, and despite the rationing, my aunts and grandmother brought the long-awaited sugar that afternoon. That's when I knew that by helping each other I was living the true meaning of Christmas.

"Gaby, pass me the sugar."

"Which one, the white or the brown sugar?"

"It doesn't matter, any will do," replied the grandmother.

"Do you want me to mix them?"

"Yes, Gaby, and you will see that it will give more flavor to the dessert."

"Yes, variety is always better," Dad said.

"Yes," said the grandmother laughing.

That night I wanted to know more and bombarded my mother with questions about the origin of St. Nicholas, and Santa Claus. Later, I learned from my mother that I bothered everyone with so many questions.

Three nights passed and each of us went down to the kitchen on separate occasions to eat Dulce Real (Royal Sweet; a dessert made with scrambled eggs and honey). My mouth still waters just imagining the eggs and honey going down my throat.

On December 24, the house looked its best. The fireplace was where we placed the Nativity, mountains made of newspaper and covered with moss (brought from the Andean mountains), a broken mirror that served as a lake and the figures painted in Italy. The Christmas

Maria Gabriela Madrid

tree had white lights, large and medium-sized angels, and a golden star at the top.

On the table was the Christmas tablecloth decorated with poinsettias, the sterling silver chargers, the white porcelain dishes with golden borders, and the colorful goblets.

It was a wonderful night on which we all wore the best costumes. While I was wearing my red dress, I never got tired of seeing myself in the mirror. Then, after midnight mass, my uncles, aunts, grandmother, and cousins came over for Christmas dinner.

I always received everything I asked of St. Nicholas and that Christmas would be no exception, but on December 25 I received something that I had not asked for in my letter. Under the tree I saw that the Christmas letter was still inside the white shoe. Also, on the table were the cookies and the glass of milk left the night before and at the nativity scene, next to the baby Jesus, was a jewelry box.

Surprised, I quickly grabbed the box, still not knowing why I was going to receive an extra gift.

Happy and naive, I longed for a ring but instead it was the blackest coal I could imagine.

Apparently, I asked a lot of questions, and the coal was for me to remember that I shouldn't ask so much.

Feeling great sadness, I cried and to this day I wonder why?

The Red Virgin

(Based on the Life of Philosopher Simone Weil)

Thanks to the advancement of technology, this time the reporter will not need a spiritualist, just by having access to the energetic platform, his molecular composition will be transformed and then appear in any plane, time and circumstance.

Without hesitation, Frederick chose to navigate through the last years of the nineteenth century and the first decades of the twentieth century. Under the inclement cold, the bells of Saint Mitchell Cathedral could be heard. Again, another move, another change that Dr. Bernard, his wife Selma and children had to face.

Selma, from a young age, knew what it was like to move, fleeing the increasingly frequent pogroms in Russia. Regularly, Jews were stoned to death under the indifferent gaze of passers-by accustomed to witnessing how the thread of life was systematically broken. Under the tutelage of a secular father and a mother clinging to Jewish customs, Selma left her dreams of being a doctor to become the wife of Dr. Bernard: Internist, intellectual and absent, who left to her the absolute responsibility of raising the children. Aimed at encouraging the children to worship the intellect, toys and sweets were forbidden in the house.

"And then what did you do to distract

yourselves?" The reporter asked, looking at Simone inquisitively.

"Andrew and I communicated in couplets. The game consisted of reciting and maintaining the right rhythm, if I got confused when reciting or lost the rhythm, Andrew would slapped me or if he was the one that lost the game, I would slapped him. We had a lot of fun."

"In what other languages did you both communicate?"

"Mostly in classical Greek. But even at twelve years of age I was fluent in other modern languages."

"How many years are there between you and Andrew?"

"Andrew is three years older than me."

"At what age did you start reading?"

"I started at an early age, and at the age of three, I was already reading the newspaper aloud."

"Coming from a privileged family, when did you feel an aversion to belonging to the elite?"

"I think since Dad was sent as a doctor to do military service. Having moved on several occasions, having left the circle of affluent families that surrounded us, made me wake up and see how other realities survived in a world convulsed by poverty. Since I was a child, I remember my aversion to materialism. When I was three years old, a relative gave me a ring and I, with great disgust, rejected it and told him that I did not like jewelry. Also, being exposed to the shortcomings of others made me despise excesses. Like when during the First World War I criticized the fact that while many did not eat, others ate in excess. I remember that at the age of six I decided to stop eating sugar because soldiers in combat lacked it."

"Was it at that same time that under the French program you adopted a soldier sent to combat?"

"Yes, and I sold wooden logs and then with the money I bought the food and clothes I sent him."

"I see your eyes moisten; did I bring back sad memories?"

"I always try not to cry in front of people, but I can't help feeling nostalgic when he visited me. It was in 1917 that he got permission to see me, we had so much fun... and to think that he died in combat a year later," she answered, while rubbing her moistened eyes with her hands."

"Having the opportunity to delve into your religious and philosophical ideas, could you comment on the path of contrasts that led you to it?"

"My life was one of changes, introspection and being exposed to the world. It itself as such was a great school for me. I think that a philosopher should not isolate from the world but rather delve into it and help others to understand other ways of thinking. I went to an elite university, then taught philosophy for a year to young women at Le Pui, and several years at Roanne. Parallel to those years of work, I organized the unemployed and the exploited to march and protest their living conditions. After that, I stopped teaching and for a year I worked at the lowest level of the French factory system: picking grapes and potatoes. I was an anarchist and a socialist, and then I criticized their ideology. I was a pacifist until I decided to stop being one. I converted to Christianity but refused to be a member of the Catholic

Maria Gabriela Madrid

Church, then went into exile in New York and then moved to London. There are so many contrasts and learnings that before continuing I would like to mention the "Allegory of the Cave."

"Could you illustrate the "Allegory of the Cave" in words?"

"Just keep in mind that the world is a Cave and that our society feeds the imagination, which is nothing more than chains, which through roles and temptations seek to chain us to distract us from the main purpose that is that through our intelligence we reach the higher plane where goodness prevails. Shadows are the passive states that we know as introspection, and shadows are the empirical knowledge acquired to make predictions, heal people, etc. Knowledge is nothing more than shadows and prisoners are those who, by allowing themselves to be manipulated, deviate from the main purpose."

"Going back to your childhood, how old were you when your love for communism began?"

"I was ten years old. At that age I was already reading different newspapers and the interest in reading communist newspapers arose. That same year I told my parents and everyone in my school that I was a Bolshevik."

"Is it true that at the age of ten you already had a penchant for history and justice?"

"History and justice were essential to me, so I suffered a lot when I learned how, through the "Treaty of Versailles" the fallen country was humiliated."

"At the age of ten, what actions did you take to ensure that justice prevailed?"

"During the holidays, in the hotel where we were

177

staying, seeing that the employees were working excessively, I gathered the bellhops, servants, assistants, doormen and urged them to form a syndicalist union."

"In fact, did you work as a trade unionist?"

"Yes, and I also taught workers, I was in demonstrations, rallies, and I even wrote in leftist newspapers."

"When did your opinion about Marxism change?"

"My criticisms of the system were exposed as soon as I entered the university."

"I understand that it was excessively criticized by the intellectual circles of the time."

"Yes, because contrary to them, I thought that political systems such as Fascism, Communism and Nationalism used force to oppress and annul the human spirit, with the aim of encouraging obedience and leaving the oppressed at the mercy of oppressors."

"Is that why you proclaimed that the essence of the human spirit must be spiritual and must be above any material need?"

"Yes, that's right. The machine must be at the mercy of the human being, and not on the contrary, the human being at the mercy of the machine."

"When did religious experiences begin and what did religious experiences lead you to?"

"I always had the desire to investigate the mystical roots of other religions, and I became a Christian."

"What was your stance on materialism?"

"I believe that by stripping ourselves of the material we are freeing ourselves from attachments. If a person voluntarily becomes a slave, not only by giving away the possessions he/she has, but by ceasing to be what he/she is, he or she is following in the footsteps of Christ and it is this hunger for God, or absolute denial of God, that causes a void, a space, that can only be filled by God."

"What was your reason for not belonging to the Catholic Church?"

"I was prevented from doing so by having to belong to a group. I was always an individualist and for me groups are harmful."

"What do you think of friendship?"

"Friendship is dangerous, it is a kind of cannibalism, because the friend becomes as necessary as food and…"

"After his death, Gustave Thibon published "Gravity and Grace" and "Necessity of Roots."

"Yes, and in them I emphasize how the material has displaced the spiritual world. As soon as we divest ourselves of the material, of the logical parts that make up the mind and let's stop being rational, lucid, is when we can reach a higher knowledge."

"What was your model of society?"

"A free society, a society where there is no oppression and that is based on respect for the human being as such, and even more so for the intrinsic right to have an eternal destiny."

"Why did you travel to Germany in 1940? What was the reason for your trip?"

"I wanted to experience with my own eyes the extent and reactions of the German population to Hitler."

"How long did you stay at Westerbrook Camp?"

"I was there for a year and from there I saw families get on the trains that would later take them to Auschwitz."

"Many question that your studies have little or nothing to do with what happened to the Jews. The fact of witnessing how they were transported to death led many to think that you would become closer to your roots. Why the silence? What happened to cause this lack of identification with the Jews? Does it have anything to do with the fact that you grew up in an assimilated family? Or that your maternal grandfather preferred not to talk about his roots? Could it be because of this that you showed surprise and dismay at the term assimilated Jew,? why "Jewish!", since the assimilated person usually has no interest in being identified with his origins?"

"Who knows…"

"Going back to when you were a child, you repeated that you were disgusting. Was this a consequence of your mother's compulsion for you to wash your hands repeatedly? Perhaps because she assumed you were disgusting from constant contact with germs?"

"I really don't know, since I was three years old, I only remember that they didn't allow people outside the house to kiss us. Only my parents, particularly my mother, did it. The phobia of germs led to an increase in the rules in the house. On one hand, it was no longer just limiting the manifestations of affection but increasing the compulsive washing of the hands. Even if Andrew happened to open the door after washing his hands during meals, he had to do it using his elbow instead of his hands."

"What reaction did your parents' friend have when he saw you?"

"Well, really what he did was to kiss my hand and I never imagined my reaction. My phobia reached such an extreme that when the doctor kissed me on the hand, I cried and screamed: water, water, I want to wash!"

"Could it be because of this that during your adolescence and adulthood you continued to reject kisses and hugs, to the point of avoiding intimate, sexual relationships? Is there any truth in that you wanted to remain chaste? Could it be because of this that you were called the "Red Virgin" at school?"

"Maybe."

"Come on, it started to drizzle," said the reporter, while grabbing her arm.

To his amazement, Simone moved her arm aggressively backwards, while staring at the reporter in a penetrating way, demanding not to do it again.

The cold seeped through their coats and the rain increased, so they walked long steps and took shelter under the columns of the back door of a coffee place.

"Are you sure you don't want to go in?"

"Yes, let's wait for it to clear and then continue. What else do you want to know?"

"I imagine you must be proud of the essays you wrote in Marseille. Would you like to name a few?"

"No, I am not proud, it is only a way for others to achieve what they must do. They were written during the time when I moved from Germany to Marseilles."

"It is believed that these works turned religious because of what you had experienced in Germany, is there any truth in that?"

"I can only tell you that some of the writings in Marseilles were "Science, Necessity and the Love of God," "Waiting for God," and others."

"When did you become involved in the dissent?"

"First when I went to Spain and fought against Franco's fascism. It was a time when I fought alongside soldiers on the front lines."

"Is it true that you never fired the rifle?"

"I didn't need to."

"Do you believe it was divine providence that intervened to cause you to stumble over the pot of hot oil left by the enemies?"

"Maybe, since after that incident I was removed from the front lines."

"And your fellow soldiers died in the struggle, would you have wished you had been with them at the time they were massacred?"

A silent environment, where Simone could be heard breathing deeply.

"Do you want to talk when you asked the French resistance to let you parachute onto French soil?"

"There is not much to say. They just didn't let me. In return, I was assigned to work reviewing papers behind a desk."

"What was the condition and reason that led you to travel with your parents to New York?"

"The reason was to escape Hitler, and the condition was that I would later go into exile in London to work under De Gaulle."

"When you went into exile in New York, what was the proposal you made to the United States government?"

"I suggested that they send nurses to the battlefield."

"And with what intention?"

"Well, so that they would provide the wounded with first aid and thus avoid death by shock or blood loss."

"Then what did you do to earn your living in London?"

"As soon as I arrived in London, I worked at De Gaulle's Freedom Organization for the French."

"Were you ill when you emigrated to London?"

"Yes, I already had tuberculosis, but I covered it up. I didn't want anything or anyone to interfere with my trip."

"I understand that despite not continuing in France, you always remained loyal to fellow soldiers in the struggle by avoiding eating more than the ration they received."

"That's how it was."

"Small portions that led your body to collapse at the end. Perhaps power struggles where you used your body to be heard? Power struggles like when you were a child."

"Are you referring to when I was recently operated on for appendicitis?"

"Yes, and your mother breastfed you for months until, due to your low weight, she decided to give you other foods as well."

"Well, the battle was hard, and it happened when I was 11 months old and refused to eat with a spoon. I lost weight and didn't grow until I was two years old when they opened holes in the bottles and mixed the food with the milk to feed me."

"What role did your mother play in your diet?"

"I believe she poisoned me with her milk and that's why I turned out to be good for nothing."

"Did you compare yourself to your brother?"

"How could I not do it if Andrew excelled since he was a child. By the age of ten he was solving advanced math problems and playing the violin like a virtuoso."

"Could you relate some of your favored antics?"

"On winter days, Andrew and I would get on the school bus without socks, our teeth shaking, and acting like we were shivering while telling people that our parents didn't feed us or take care of us. We always asked for candy because it was forbidden at home."

"Returning to the use of your body as a means of protest, on more than one occasion when you were with your parents you only ate what you could afford."

"Even when I was with them, I did not stop suffering for others. It was through those episodes that I made them see the hunger that our soldiers were going through on the battlefront."

"Did you ever regret taking your body to the extreme of starvation or anorexia? or does it rather have to do with the fact that you wanted to reach the supreme state within the Cathar belief of committing suicide by letting yourself die of starvation?"

"I died at 34 years old and for me it was a long life," she replied, shaking off her rain-soaked coat while coughing nonstop.

"Would you be willing to die again, as Christ did for all of us?"

"As a final comment, I want you to know that I have envied Christ every time I look at Him crucified and I will continue to do so."

"Simone de Beauvoir admired more than your condition as a philosopher, your ability to feel the suffering of others."

"Yes, she was amazed when I cried about the famine unleashed in China."

"Regarding those years as university classmates, was there any rivalry between you two?"

"I only remember that I was the one who acquired the best grades."

"And now, returning to your deathbed, what is the truth in the speculation that you were baptized at the last minute?"

"It is well known that despite wanting to live the sacraments, the position of not being a member of the Catholic Church was more powerful in me."

"An anarchist Catholic?"

"Call it what you want, but there are also several speculations: The first, that I consented to be baptized, or the second, that I was baptized while I was unconscious. Really for those who knew me, the answer was obvious."

"What are you doing? Are you going to smoke?"

"Don't be alarmed, I can't die twice. Smoking is only a habit, for having passed after my death into an ethereal state I no longer feel any pleasure."

Simone, slim-faced and wearing a gray suit, raised her hand and said goodbye, showing a tired face as she walked with long strides toward the Ashford-Kent Sanatorium, her final resting place.

Seeking the Truth

The time had come, he had to risk what before was considered impossible. A dark living room, dimly lit by candles. Songs of those present anticipate the splitting of the spiritualist. For moments it will serve as a vehicle for the journalist, his voice will be different, hoarse, and his gestures will be delicate. Icy currents will anticipate the moment when the journalist will be sucked in and taken to the afterlife.

"Excuse me, but while I was being sucked through the tunnel a condensed cloud disheveled my hair."

"I understand."

"Yes, I only mention it because I see you drinking your orange juice, and those booksellers, what books do they contain?"

"Stories and magazines."

"I see, there are your favorites by Charles May." Excuse me, what does that urn contain?"

"Ashes, and it's not just that, there are several scattered as you can see, replied to the reporter while looking at his wristwatch. I think it's better to start once and for all because at any moment they will come to pick you up to escort you back."

"Okay, let's begin. Is this your vicinity?"

"Yes, although I am not subject to staying here, I can also go down to other levels."

"Like which ones?"

"Where my companions- in- struggle are: Himmler and Mengele. You know Mengele made great progress in his experiments when he was in Brazil."

"Well, you're talking about the small town of German generations where the percentage of twins is more than forty percent."

"Yes, that's right."

"That has not yet been proven. It must be a coincidence. Tell me, how do your days go?"

"During the day I read and paint."

"Do you still paint?"

"Yes, architectural sketches, a product of Germany's greatness and the levels around me."

"Do I imagine that you will see women and men copulating?"

"Yes, and there are places to witness them."

"And those barracks? Do they belong to a concentration camp?"

"Well, keep in mind that anything is possible here, which is why the concentration camps are within walking distance of each other. The one you see is Auschwitz."

"And that Wagnerian aria, is it one of your favorites?"

"That's right."

"Many historians think that you identified with the composer and not precisely because of his genius."

"It was really because of his excellence both in music and in writing."

"You rather mean because of racism, arrogance. I can even say that you both identified by the uncertainty of your origins."

Annoyed by the insinuation, he cast a fixed, piercing, cold glance at the obtrusive journalist.

"It is better not to get ahead of ourselves and continue with your childhood."

"Everything has been said", he replied, irritated as he got up from his chair.

"Perhaps you are right, because there have been many books and films aimed at you, but there are details that, taking advantage of this unusual interview, I would like to have the opportunity to clarify. You will see that I can be your most faithful collaborator. Do you think that the constant changes of housing influenced your inability to show or feel empathy towards others?"

"What do you mean?"

"I've never had problems with empathy, and it is true that we moved seven times to be exact; and attended five different schools."

"Don't you think that so much change influenced your apathy to relate intimately to others? Could it be that your actions were a representation of what others expected to receive from you, and that you did feel joy in seeing people's suffering?"

"Whose, of the inferior ones?"

"Of the sub-human race, as you call it."

"For this reason, because they were sub-human they did not deserve my attention, much less my empathy. They brought misery and shame to our homeland and what I did was to try to make the dream resurface with force, because you know that, as List and Liebenfels implied, our people descended from the Aryan superior race that survived the disappearance of Atlantis. That is why I tried to preserve its purity, to

Maria Gabriela Madrid

forbid pure German blood to mix with inferior people. That's why I decided to put an end to them."

"Is that why you wanted to get rid of the handicapped, the gypsies, the Jews and the mentally disabled? Or did your rejection rather come from your own genetics, from people around you with mental retardation and madness? Did that fear of intimacy have to do with the fear of bringing mentally disabled beings into the world?"

"I don't know what you are talking about. In my family there has always been pure blood."

Journalist's note: He cannot recognize that there was madness and mental retardation among his relatives.

"And what about your sister?"

"What about her?"

"She hid whenever your childhood friend visited the house. Apparently, she did not come out. Was she hiding or was she hidden?"

"She hid. Those were things from childhood."

"Going back to your inability to be intimate and a study of your body language…"

"Again, that Freud. He knows I don't believe in him."

"How do you explain your gesture of placing your hands in front of you to cover your private part? Maybe to cover the fact that it had an incomplete development?"

"That's nonsense."

"You know that when you are one of them, sexual energy is transferred to the gaze. Could it be that the reason your gaze is penetrating, cold and indolent?"

Silence. There was no response.

"Returning to your similarities with Wagner, both of you never knew the origin of your parents and the fear of being Jewish caused both to hate and reject everything related to the Jewish culture. Is it true that Wagner was the first to mention the possibility that there were no Jews?"

"Yes, he mentioned it in his anti-Semitic writings, but I was the one that made it happened."

"When you were in power, did you get answers about your father's origins? Why did they destroy the church coffers, and other documents? Was your father Jewish? Do you have Jewish blood in your veins?"

"Where are you going with that?"

"I am the one asking the questions."

"And I am the one who answers them."

"Remember this is your chance to get your message across."

"My blood is pure. I am the greatest representative of the Aryan race."

"How do you assert that, when on the scale of physical examinations, you are not tall, blond, blue-eyed? In short, it is even rumored that you grew your mustache to hide the inclination of your nose. It is also said that for a period of time your father had the maternal name Schicklgruber and it was after she married that your father change his last name to Hitler. If your father had not changed the maternal surname, Schicklgruber, you would not have had the reach you had in military service and you would have had difficulty getting thousands and millions of people to shout Heil Schicklgruber instead of Heil Hitler. Wasn't that why the change of your surname? Your father from being an illegitimate son to a legitimized one…"

Getting up, he threw the chair and walked in circles, mute, without giving an answer.

"How true is it that you always felt protected from misfortunes?"

"Well, since I was a child, I saw how my brothers died at a young age, leaving only me as a survivor, and I always knew that I was protected and destined to fulfill a great mission. And about my sister, you know…"

"Yes, of course, being a woman she was inferior to you. Every woman is inferior to man, exclusively with the mission of being pretty and to be able to procreate."

"That's right."

"Is that why you never bothered to give your mother a Christian burial? What do you have to say about the years it was without a tombstone?"

"Those were years in which there was not enough money."

"But how do you say that, if even after your father passing, you all lived a life without hardships…"

"Silence."

"From your time as a teenager, what experience would you have liked to change?"

"None, because they all led me to what I am."

"Perhaps, having been rejected by the Vienna Academy of Arts? It is known that you made two attempts to be accepted."

"Those infamous people got their comeuppance. They were inferior. Do you know that of the seven judges, four were Jews?"

"Is it true that you avoided intellectuals so as not to feel less capable. It is known that you only read racist supplements of dubious origin and children's stories. Why was there nothing in your library of books on philosophy, literature, etc?"

"Certainly, you have been misinformed."

"And what about seeing your friend Kubizek (whom you considered inferior) graduating with honors in Music from the Vienna Conservatory? And you, who never finished your formal education, and still writes in childish handwriting, like a schoolboy. Is that why at the time you were Fuher, you always surrounded yourself with intellectually inferior beings so that they would not question you?"

"Again, the contained rage was expressed through his gaze."

"Your companions during First World War commented on the excessive care you took with your weapon, did you revere it, and protect it?"

"It was the one I used to fight and gain ground during the war. Those infamous German traitors who surrendered and did not want to continue fighting."

"Are you talking to me about the First World War?"

"Yes, and it was those shoddy colonels and generals who accepted the infamous conditions of the Treaty of Versailles."

"Is that why you were eager to form your own political party in the post-war period?"

"Yes, because the one destined to save the working class had few followers. There were about 60 members."

"Yes, and you were member number 55, although they later gave you the number 7 position for the rest to believe that you were with the organization from the beginning."

"True, and I decided to continue with them because my speeches attracted more followers. You know how they surrendered at my feet!"

"If what you wanted was the well-being of your people, why didn't you surrender in time to avoid the destruction of your country? Why drag the people into misery, disillusionment and death?"

"I gave all the sacrifice for my country, and they had to stay with me until the end. I only regretted not finishing them all."

"At the time of committing suicide, did you feel any regret? What did you feel when you saw Eva die? Did you remember your cousin Gilde, who died in the same way? And about Gilde, is it true that she killed herself because you cut short her dreams of being an artist, of going in search of her own destiny? Was it true that you controlled even the clothes she had to wear?"

Uncomfortable, he omitted an answer, taking a handkerchief from his pocket with which he began to clean the furniture around him.

"I see that your mania for cleanliness is true."

"Everything must shine."

Ironic comment from the journalist: "Yes, as you shone before the fall".

"What fall?"

Once again, the journalist is astonished at the lack of recognition of his crimes against humanity.

"What do you think of the attitude of some to think that you Nazis were solely responsible for the right-wing extremism experienced in the country?"

"In fact, long ago, before the First World War, anti-Semitic pamphlets were already circulating, and pogroms occurred frequently. In Russia, murders took place in the middle of the street, under the support and silence of so many of the passers-by who chose not to intervene."

"Do you feel that the environment was given for your movement to emerge? An environment where, after the First World War, the poverty and variability of the currency showed how before you bought a loaf of bread for 165 Marks and by the end of the year the same piece of bread was one million five hundred thousand Marks."

"That's right, Great Germany had succumbed to the monopolies of the Jews."

"With an expression of disgust, but remembering his position as a journalist, he limited himself to not answering what was mentioned and decided to ask again."

"Much is said about the several pills they gave you. Is it true that it changed your personality?"

"No. They were just vitamins."

"Do you mean amphetamines?"

"They gave me strength and energy."

"What is your opinion of occultism? And what role did it play in the government?"

"Look, they are coming for you."

"How come? It barely have passed 20 min?"

"That will be where you come from, but two hours have passed here."

"I see, it's different."

"Notice that for those on the other side, it should be hot here, and no, rather the intense cold is what preserves us to one day return and finish what we started."

The reporter looks at him aggrievedly.

"What do they think of me?"

"Of you, that you were a megalomaniac, hysterical, mad, demon and…"

"Enough! enough! You are lying. I know that there are those who admire me."

"Let's say that there are, but they are a minority."

Intense cold, icy currents mark the moment of suction when the journalist reaches the other side and leaves the spiritist's body.

A room with the lights off, curtains closed, where only by being attentive to humanity must we make sure it does not happen again.

Pomponia

I never imagined having such a special friendship. She was very loyal for years, always sharing that daily hour of walking, willing to give affection and be available at the most difficult moments of solitude, night or day, so I always felt that I could count on her. Presumptuous and flirtatious, she hated exaggerated haircuts. On more than one occasion she was a victim of the merciless action of the scissors, so she preferred to hide, and no one would see her if she was not wearing her impeccable fur coat.

On Christmas night, everyone in the house wore their best clothes and Pomponia was not far behind when she wore her cream-colored fur coat and the blue taffeta bow, placed on her side, gave her an aristocratic air, in tune with that of her ancestors, nobility of the Tibetan empire, whose perennial coat literally covered her entire body that in tropical weather suffered from heat, but her instinct for adventure was more powerful when she enjoyed those boat rides to the beaches of Morrocoy, Venezuela. Intense in character, she was always the first to jump into the water.

Curiously, one afternoon her belly began to bulge. No one knew her partner, apparently, he was older than her. Fortunately, the quintuplets were born without problems, only with the misfortune of having Pomponia as a mother. She rejected them, tried not to feed them and terrified of the responsibility of being a mother, she disappeared for several days. I remember everyone in the house looking for her, shouting her name, notifying anyone who might have seen her, until weeks later, she returned covered in the dust of the construction site near the house, tired and panting for water.

Life went on without major surprises until the day Pomponia chose to end it. Having witnessed the intention to give her away, she precipitated her suicide. Pomponia would not resist moving away from those she loved, so without listening to warnings, she threw herself into the street. Several cars dodged her, while growling, with moist eyes, she prevented anyone from approaching her, until that fateful blue car, like its taffeta bow, crushed her entrails. Far from her lost kingdom, the strange lands of Tibet, the faithful and joyful Pomponia, died in Venezuela.

Lusitano

Lusitano is locked up. Unlike his ancestors, those Mustangs that rode free day and night exposed to sudden changes in temperature, he is under a controlled environment and a strict routine. At dawn he is taken to the riding circle to drink water and eat grass. Algiro, the one in charge of brushing him, places the rein, saddle and stirrups to tame him. Of all the hundreds of horses received, Lusitano is the most difficult to tame because his blood still runs with the energy of wild horses. Unlike the Mustangs that once were the owners and lords of the mountains, since they modified the law that previously protected them, recently ten thousand horses were sent to European territory for consumption, and wild horses are now part of the endangered species.

Hundreds of descendants of the Mustangs neigh day and night. With unbridled gallop they try to flee from the raids carried out by the cowboys, who invade their lands, seeking to corner them to deprive them of freedom. Cowboys who, with the help of helicopters and loudspeakers, carry out the maneuvers required to take them to the vicinity of the prison, where, locked in a corral, they receive daily visits from the inmates. The government program uses them in the rehabilitation of prisoners for the purpose of that with daily contact and care, the beast (man) develops the empathy necessary to live in society. Months in which Algiro is the only one who has daily contact with Lusitano. Algiro, due to

Maria Gabriela Madrid

Lusitano's good behavior, has been working with animals for two years, his previous experience as a rancher warns him that Lusitano's surly attitude must be moderate.

Algiro, condemned to spend his days between cold walls, has no hope of regaining his freedom and knows that Lusitano will spend his days imprisoned in a barnyard. He would be tamed, carrying limestone stones in his leather bags for hours so that investors with their expansionist ideas can build various developments. Projects that will obstruct the beauty of the natural landscape with their concrete. An arid land, where the stillness of the night is broken by the moans and neighs of the unfortunate.

On an April afternoon, Algiro lost the battle. Many were the failed attempts and because he could not tame Lusitano he was taken out of the corral to be sold or sent to the slaughterhouse. The fate of so many others that, when they were not bought, ended up being meat for dogs, while their resistant leather rests on the backs of other horses. Lusitano was restless on the morning of the transfer. The foreman in charge paraded it before potential buyers, while in the distance, Algiro closed the fence so that the new group of horses could not escape.

First, the second and third rounds were Lusitano was not chosen. Algiro, moved, remembered the failed attempts at training, the surly caresses and the vitality and energy of the wild horse. Contriving not to be taken to the slaughterhouse, Algiro lifted the handle of the fence and shouted to distract the attention of the cowboys, while Lusitano, spirited, kicked the foreman and sent him swiftly to the ground, and rising on two legs, neighing, charged with all the horses that crossed his path.

Meanwhile, Algiro, happy to see him free, returned to the prison to report that the group of horses had escaped.

The Shiny Star

Luminaria is a place where tourists and passers-by can experience all five senses of plenitude. When Teresita went inside the Convention Center, colorful paintings ignited her imagination. It was a night for her to vibrate to the sound of classical music, to imagine herself as a storyteller, or to allow the story to transport her to another dimension, where life and death share the same time and space.

The seven stages of Luminaria embraced hope and willingness of artists to entertain anyone.

Teresita was really amazed, and with her eyes wide open, she couldn't wait to read all the poems on the wall, to dance to the beat of merengue and to the beat of Mark Anthony, to imitate ballet, modern dance, hip hop or even dance at her own rhythm.

Every move and every cheer of happiness were allowed within safe boundaries. Police officers were everywhere, giving people extra help: "Wait, come this way, or no speak Spanish, but wait is that way."

For one evening, Teresita felt she was on stage all the time, and from The Shining Tents to Las Pampas-Argentina, she couldn't wait to watch the Tango dancers. By impulse, she ran with all her might, and with her adrenaline at the highest point, she passed long lines of people waiting for salty pretzels, hot dogs, hamburgers, and gyros, until a noise roared in her stomach stopped her suddenly. Teresita was in front of tacos, Chalupas and carnitas, and needed to eat to sustain her big belly.

Hungry as she was, she could not wait in those long lines, and counting her coins, she realized she didn't have enough money to buy a peanut.

Teresita has been unemployed for a while, but now that she was distracted by the festival of Green Lights, her economic situation was not relevant anymore. Like someone with a premonition, she envisioned herself as Miss Teresita, the cook, and without wasting any time, she grabbed a white tablecloth to cover her purple-t-shirt and tied her hair in a long ponytail.

"Muchacha, where were you? We thought you would never come, and we need your help. There are too many people in line. What is your name?"

"Teresita."

"Come on and start making chalupas. I will make more tortillas, and Chariot will make tacos."

Time passed, and Teresita, behind everybody's back, ate carnitas, chalupas and tacos. Excited at getting paid and ready to walk down the streets, Teresita, without being noticed, folded her dirty sheet and slowly disappeared among tourists and passers-by.

Luminaria was a magical festival, where for a short time, Teresita forgot about being unemployed, and went from a common girl, to performer, and to a shiny star.

Maria Gabriela Madrid

Lactivore

"Several months have passed since the three of us walked along the Hudson River and while you and I were distracted watching the coast of New Jersey, Ramirito smelled and held in his hands that flower never seen before. Do you remember, with the purple center and the three velvety crimson petals? I understand that Ramirito would have wanted to grab that flower due to their contrasts but breathed that putrid smell, why didn't you grab the flower?"

"Oh Alicia, you already know that it was when he touched it and breathed in the fragrance that started it all. We can no longer do anything but try to protect our identity."

"As you say, but you must do something, not even nine gallons of milk a day are enough. Diego: his bone structure does not increase in length but in density. Ramirito does not chew, he swallows."

"Well, Alicia, at least the molecules in his body don't turn into fat cells. It is already incredible that it automatically maintains its anatomy and transforms what is necessary into pure energy. Don't worry, Alicia, and get ready, Central Park is waiting for us."

Months later, now sitting, remembering, I write what happened. I'll never forget the magnitude of that stroll by Central Park. Japanese trees displaying the pink flowers to the fullest. Children play soccer and on the other side children play baseball. Strollers of babies,

203

men, women, and the elderly enjoying the sunny April afternoon. Any afternoon in which Ramirito, even for a day, wanted to be like the others. Without us noticing, in seconds he was no longer walking next to us. Nervous, but determined to find him, you put on your mask to avoid recognition, while I used a blue-green cloth to cover my face, leaving only my eyes visible.

I focused my eyes and like a camera, my brain activated the zoom lens, and I captured that Ramirito was among those on the soccer team. I thought that without a uniform and with his face covered, the rest of the children were not going to let him play, but the ball crossed the field at such a speed that when Ramirito saw it, without knowing the rules of the game, he intercepted it in the air. Witnesses said he jumped several feet to catch it.

Amazed by his agility, the coaches wanted to have him on their team. The children who made up the team no longer counted, because for that day Ramirito ran, deflected the ball and, goal after goal, gave the team the victory. At the end of the cheers, he ran to the baseball field and waved the bat to hit the grass many times until he realized how the game was being played.

Ramirito quickly hit a home run and, running at lightning speed, brought the win to the Mini Yankees.

Heated, the mask was itchy, but he could not take it off. You watched his every move until suddenly the window-worker was hanging from the building.

From the heights there were shouts, sobs, and pleas in Spanish, when suddenly Ramirito stretched and sat up and flew away to the sixteenth floor, from where he straightened the scaffolding and with superhuman strength stopped the worker's fall.

"Do you remember, Diego, the applause, and the cheers? Everyone cheered Ramirito on as he slowly laid the scaffolding with the young man almost fainting on the concrete."

Now I know that day was important in our lives, because from that moment on we stopped being a normal family. From then on, for months, we always hid our identity and Ramirito played the hero, saving whoever was in misfortune, until that afternoon when he heard the fateful news that the imported milk was contaminated.

I know that is why you both went to the port, because you wanted to stop any shipments coming from China. Diego, I know that you tried to get Ramirito to avoid tasting it, but he managed to get not the nine gallons a day that he used to, but the sixteen that he needed until that moment.

Diego, I can simply tell you that I admire how you put your life at risk by showing him the danger he was in.

I was disturbed to know that it was you who took every gallon of milk that arrived from China to rule out the milk being tainted, and it was until the thirteenth that your stomach could not handle one more drink and you let it pass.

Oh Diego, dismayed I am still sitting here, remembering, and writing what happened.

Mrs. Pia showed me the video in which you go out with Ramirito in the port, to be more precise, the Wal-Mart cameras located on Jackson's corner were the ones that captured when you refused to taste the thirteenth gallon and shows how Ramirito, when taking his first sip, witnesses his skin turned blue. You must have had a great impression when you realized that the milk didn't give him strength, but on the contrary, caused Ramirito to convulse and, after hours of vomiting, he threw out all the milk, one-hundred gallons accumulated since he smelled that flower in his hands.

Now that I have you face to face, in this bronze urn, I can tell you that after drowning, Ramiro's body decomposed. The effect of the poisoned milk with the components of that damned flower caused his molecules to be activated and the previously positive energy reduced it to ashes. In Queens, there was no flooding, but reports indicated that buildings and houses were underwater in Manhattan. I know that you and Ramirito were only looking to help and that is why I feel this deep sadness to see how you both caused such an outcome.

Now, as the only survivor of the family, I deposit my greenish-blue cloth and this letter in the rings of your chamber. Goodbye beloved Diego, and I only hope that it will be a long time before we see each other again.

Maria Gabriela Madrid

The Vampire's Basket

The day arrived and with a suitcase in hand she boarded the 747 airplane that would take her to New Orleans. The city of myths and legends that required her talent. The crimes considered normal (to kill someone to steal a wallet), were conducted without any imagination. The crimes take place in the streets or on any sidewalk at any time of the day. But what happened lately was beyond the sadism of the psychopath, or perhaps as some said the sadism of vampires that, eager for blood, nailed their fangs in the necks of their victims, leaving them among the garbage bags in cemeteries or perhaps as the last crime reported on the banks of the Mississippi river.

The purpose of Elise's new work is to shed light on the dark campaign that discredited the city.

More than one scandalous newspaper published the photos, some altered, others not, of the corpses, and as a result, tourism had fallen in exorbitant numbers, causing an economic crisis that led to restaurants with decades in service to close and hotels lowering their prices because of the competition with the Airbnb apartments and houses that did not allow them to charge traditional rates.

Elise would work for the company "City Public Relations or CPR," that had restored the trust of tourists to visit Florida, full of sharks and criminals. Common agents that tourists now view as part of the state's fauna.

The assigned apartment was located downtown

so that it would be closer to any place that she wanted to visit. She had just begun the first day of work when the desk had already spread out the last photographs of the crimes that had taken place.

Many commons crimes and one that stood out. The forty-year-old man covered in rocks that was spotted by tourists returning from their journey of the Mississippi river aboard the steamboat "Natchez." A Steamboat that entertains during the day with the wind organ and during the night with the jazz band and buffet included.

A voyage that promised moments of tranquility and delight, but on the contrary, ended with the bloody reality of death, that some die before, and others later, some die peacefully, or others violently, as the executive whose pale head showed a hole in his brain where the criminal would have eaten, or taken his brain as a trophy, and in his neck the mark of two fangs where the blood of the victim would have been extracted.

The second photo of the newspaper showed the matches between the fingers of his already paralyzed hand. Because of the maroon color and golden letters, Elise presumes that it probably was from the bar "Galatoire's 33 Bar and Steak," located on Bourbon Street. Memories of when she was with her daughter tasting the filet mignon with a glass of French red wine. The sober decoration of the restaurant, those seats of brown leather and the tables of cedar wood. Elise longed to have her again at her side, but she knew that while the job was temporary, she would not be available to offer the required security.

"It is a pleasure to meet you Elise Smith, I am

your boss, Frederick Bloom. I am coming to tell you that we are waiting to welcome you in the conference room."

Without haste, Elise removed her glasses, and following her boss, entered the room. A moment that would establish the camaraderie with her boss and new colleagues who supported, opposite of her, the existence of ghosts, demons, vampires, zombies, or any other kind that inhabited the subworld.

"Just by looking at this welcoming basket I think I need supernatural guidance to understand it", said Elise while laughing loudly.

The wicker basket with gray strands of hair, broken fingernail, a doll of African clothing, a black bag and an invitation to the Halloween party.

"Sure, you would think that nothing in the basket has powers. It is always the same with the majority that come from outside, but believe me it is true, said Frederick, her boss. Just look at the death of the one you are investigating. The police think the killer may have been a vampire."

Thanking them for the gesture, Elise left, and carrying the basket was tempted to leave it in the dumpster but decided not to hurt the feelings of her boss and colleagues and took it to her apartment.

The collective spirit of the city felt full during the foggy days. And that afternoon, due to the thick fog, the visibility was low and among the nooks of the streets Elise heard songs that she had never heard before and screams that made it speed up to get to the building soon.

A building that represented the past glory and decadence of the city and that, instead of gentleman with black top hats depositing their money in "The First

National Bank of Commerce," were the pieces of the plaster cornices, and the holes in the marble walls showed what happened after the precipitous fall of the market, the countless suicides and the millions of impoverished people. It was the depression of 1929, and now, with some restoration of the marble walls and glass chandeliers, the purpose was to hide that past.

Elise's apartment had high ceilings, plaster cornices, and on one side the enviable view of the Mississippi river, and the streets of the French Quarter, and on the other side, the Orthodox Church that alternated between Catholic, Protestant and Orthodox masses and, in its eagerness to increase assistance of the faithful, it counted sometimes with the participation of the choir of the church, of sopranos, or the organist who played baroque music.

Every Sunday, the chimes of the church a block away from the building reminded her of the daily masses at her school and the Sunday masses she attended growing up. They were chimes that she heard as she walked in front of the church when the warning cry of the homeless man who, barefoot and lying on his side, shouted: "In New Orleans the vamps only enter the houses if they are invited, but Belial, Samael, Lucifer, Mephistopheles or Satan and we his disciples, are in the streets! We wander the streets!"

At the same time, he compulsively scratched his forearm and tripped while making the gesture of shooting down anyone who crossed his path. Elise dodged him, accelerated her pace and walked the streets in her eagerness to feed on the magic of the city and in broad daylight she saw Death dressed as Katrina, pirates, magicians, singers, jazz players, and the African American woman of the clarinet that with her talent she would have full attendance at the Carnegie Hall. Elise, inspired, spent weeks on the creation of the campaign. Dozens of drawings showing the angelic face of a vampire baby tasting small pieces of meat and at the tip of his fang the drop of blood slipping on the slogan, "The Vampire in me". Announcements that would certainly be at Prime Meat' restaurants. Also, ads narrating the vampires' good acts: Stopping the overflowing water of the Mississippi with its cape, Vampires catching in the act the murderous vampires who in cages would disappear at sunrise, announcements of vampires drinking in the bars and with the tip of their layer covering the drinks so they won't be altered, vampires showing shining smiles to generate confidence. Vampires assisting with street crossing. Vampires driving the trams. In short, a campaign that, by showing them doing daily tasks, would restore empathy with humans and bring back lost confidence. The presentation in Power Point in colors was ready and it was only necessary to get the Victorian custom for the day of the presentation, because as promoter of the campaign, Elise would go disguised as a vampire. Frederick, delighted with the idea, took her to the busiest warehouse during Mardi-Gras.

"Here it is Elise, this one is perfect commented Frederick while lifting it to not drag it. Look, it is red taffeta-like blood as you wanted it and with black lace. Also, the black taffeta overskirt contrasts with the red bodice and white lace sleeves. It is spectacular, as if it was made for you."

Yes, it is! I will buy it and then I will try it on at the apartment, otherwise we won't have time to get to the appointment.

"Are you sure it does not hurt?"

"I guess it's just getting used to it."

The entrance led to a dark and dirty corridor. The pungent odor of dried blood and burned blood disturbed Elise until she had to sit in the dentist's chair. The semi-transparent plastic fangs came in large, medium and small and Elise chose the medium ones, and the sharp ends of the fangs were molded.

On the day of the presentation, she wore her Victorian costume and won the approval of the team. Frederick and Elisa went to the restaurant "Galatoire's 33 Bar and Stake, to celebrate. Frederick laughs while seeing Elise's fangs covered in red blood that came from piercing the piece of meat and reminded him of the vampire baby of the campaign.

"You are already baptized! Now you cannot taste anything that is not blood. Ha ha ha."

"Ha ha nothing, those are myths, Frederick. Nothing more than that. You cannot believe in vampires."

Leaving the restaurant with their drinks in hand, they walked through Bourbon, Canal and Baronne Streets until they reached the building illuminated with purple and yellow lights.

Inside the apartment the basket was there for them to play the game of vampires, and Elise took the black bag and, untying the tie, ignored the pleas of Frederick and with the black cloth on the table invoked the vampire. Between the mocking laughter and her gaze fixed on the cloth Elise saw the central flower and the symbols that surrounded it and read aloud "Nades, Suradis, Maniner."

Frederick, stunned, saw how a thick mist appeared in the center of the apartment and took a human sinister form. The pallor of his skin contrasted with his black suit and white fangs eager for new blood.

Rubbing his eyes Frederick saw that it was not a hallucination. To subdue and dominate the vampire Elise read aloud "Sader, Prostas, Solaster". In fractions of seconds Elise and the vampire looked at each other and closed the pact and Frederick shocked, tried to hide, but the speed of the vampire anticipated his steps. From behind, the vampire embraced Frederick's neck and twisting, it nailed the fangs in and drinking the hot blood took the strength to tear, to open with his fingernails, the skull and to eat the brains while Elise removed the makeup, the plastic fangs and place the black cloth with the one she used before arriving in New Orleans.

Elise in pajamas gave the order, and at the speed of thunder the vampire took the corpse and threw it behind the garbage bags of the building. The vampire evaporated in a gray-brown haze until the next time Elise would invoke him, perhaps at the Halloween party where the vice-president of City Public Relations (CPR) would be present.

Erika

The magic was impregnated in the air. It was the intermixed odors of the rum, of the whiskey, the beer of the impromptu drinks in the hands of the passers-by who, without looking, walked through the streets that gave off the smells of fresh and old urine. That unmistakable fragrance of dusty streets that were sometimes disinfected with soap and water.

Erika was lying between the white sheets. She tried to get up and could not, she felt the heaviness of her body and again, another failed attempt. She wanted to get up and see what was the excitement and laughter that filtered through the walls of the apartment. After splitting herself in two, she flew over the streets and saw young addicts in front of the churches, in the corners and in the middle of the sidewalks waiting for money or food; black bags of garbage posted in the streets, in full view, and the chiffon dress inlaid with colored stones on the black bag that was still there, intact as if no one had worn it.

Without thinking she timidly touched it, felt the stones and grabbed it while going to the restaurant across the street to change inside the bathroom. Tied to her body, Erika saw her reflection in the mirror and noticed that her white complexion had turned black, and her hair was not loose but in braids. The only thing that remained the same was the semi-transparent dress of shining stones. Dazed, she sat down at the bar and fixed her gaze on the color of her hands until screams and shoves made her wobble. Confused, she looked at them and saw only hatred and anger towards her. They pushed her and threw her out of the restaurant, tearing her dress. The screams continued and among the crowd she saw young people who were persecuted, about to be lynched. They spoke differently and their skin was cinnamon colored. Erika, hidden behind the column, witnessed how one by one, they were killed, and remembered the reports when African Americans were hanged in the adjacent plantations.

She dried her tears with the tip of her dress when she spotted carriages instead of cars, and the mansion; the empty house that survived the flames that escaped through its windows, witness of the captivity and dismemberment of the slaves and the baths that Madame Marie Delphine LaLaurie took with the blood that she extracted from the slaves and that she thought would return the freshness to her skin.

The opulent parties in the Mansion of the Count of Saint Germaine, the delicacies and bottles of wine that after the denunciation of the bite that the Count gave to the maid and the immediate disappearance of the Count, revealed that some of the wine bottles were mixed with human blood.

The dark narrow streets of the French Quarter witness beings that move or stop waiting for the bait. Night in which Erika saw a woman with the sharp tip of her teeth showing a semi-smile.

Stories of vampires, witchcraft and the power achieved in the political arena by Marie Laveau, the Queen of Voodoo. The loud sound of the drums and the howls of the animals when they were sacrificed in exchange for favors. The outdoor rituals of the sacrifice of the chicken, of the corn offering to share with people. Black magic and white magic. The welcome gift, without sender, that Erika received in her apartment. The little doll with African clothes that she placed in the center of the table. A doll that marked the beginning of the rest of her days. They said that it was at the end of her visit that she already had the material required for her dissertation when someone crossed her path and spit on her face. Her symptoms were the cough that became permanent, the sudden weight loss, the cold sweats and the spit full of blood on the bowl at the edge of the bed. White sheets that contrasted with the paleness of her white skin. Her body without strength and her languid gaze bet that the end was near. Friends and family members commented that she was semi-unconscious, that she babbled tales of lynchings and vampires, and that her little strength was clinging to the doll in African clothing.

A doll that was snatched after her death, and that by removing the African dress was a red "X" in the site of the lungs. The lifting of her body was silent. Her mother and her aunts washed her and dressed her in the dress chosen by her mother, the chiffon dress inlaid with precious stones that gave life to her face, and canvas without folds, without wrinkles waiting to be made up. The mourners' whining could be heard before they exited their apartment onto the street, where the horse-drawn carriage was prepared to transport her to the cemetery.

Musicians with black top hats played slow, melancholic jazz, joined by family and friends waving white handkerchiefs and spinning colorful umbrellas. The cheerful jazz then celebrated Erika's life.

Maria Gabriela Madrid

Procession that under the thread of rain paraded through Baronne, Canal, Jackson Square, the streets of the French Quarters to the cemetery where those present witnessed the funeral.

Erika's mother was inconsolable and refused to leave her. The chosen night, the movement of the leaves broke the silence of the cemetery and forming a semi-circle, Erika's mother saw how the priestess was contorted and between songs and invocations, ordered Erika to wake up from the deep sleep that was death.

Night of thunder and lighting and the storm that announced that dead and alive are living together in the square, in the streets, in the bars, in the corners and posted on the lantern the strong and tall man played the trumpet. The man that had a broad smile and deep voice. Melancholic tunes that blurred the African rhythms that interspersed with lyric and improvised sounds told the sadness and joy of life.

Jackson Square, where different bands play jazz every day, music from the Mississippi, the blues of slavery, the persecutions and lynchings carried out by people hidden in hooded white sheets, casual loves and truncated lives. Bands competing for the attention of tourists.

Children and young people dancing in the streets. The young, shy, self-absorbed but attentive young man that narrates what happens around him and Erika who wanders and shines in her chiffon dress and shiny stones. Erika, the pale-faced Katrina with contours outlined by vivid colors, that friendly waves to Louis, who played his trumpet, and William who writes as Erika watched as her gown of glittering stones was touched and admired

217

The Dance of the Shadows

by the newly arrived tourists to wait for the daring one
that would cross the threshold and return to wander with
them the dark narrow streets of the city.

Strings

When I attended the annual physics conference, I was amazed at the possibility of the existence of other universes, where not only do the already established three dimensions of space and time exist, but a cluster of eleven dimensions imperceptible to the human eye.

The theory called "Strings" states that each organism, regardless of its size and whether it is perceived or not, has the filaments of the molecules required to be in the dance of life.

These filaments, formed by energy, vibrate in different ways, so if the theory were to be proven, it would finally allow the unification of Quantum Mechanics and the Theory of Relativity.

Also at the conference, as part of quantum mechanics, the fantasy of the existence of several universes was mentioned, perhaps in parallel planes? Who knows.

What a pleasure it would be to be able to see beyond and not remain static in this universe where only chaos, wars and evil are glimpsed.

I rarely make decisions that have been influenced by premonitions, coincidences or strange situations; I remember that time, when after a day of work, I was resting on the terrace of the house, and suddenly a growing anguish pressed on my chest. I thought for a moment about Marta, and I sensed that she was unwell and was crying. There was no reason to worry, but despite that I still called her home.

The phone line was busy all the time so I took the keys to my yellow Volkswagen, (adored sixties clunker that even in the nineties was an accomplice of my outings), and arriving at Marta's house, I saw Gonzalo in the garden, who desperately, walking in circles, cell phone in hand, was looking for a nanny to take care of the children. Finally, he answered me and in a broken voice told me that Marta had just died at the intersection located three blocks from the house. I had no more information, only that the accident had occurred ten minutes before my arrival, in the brief time that I was calling Marta from my house and her phone line was busy while Gonzalo answered the call of the police inspector. With goosebumps, I understood that Marta, at that moment of dying, was saying goodbye to me. With no other help to offer, I sobbed and drove to the garage of my house. Years passed and that episode remained forever in my memory. Now, in the kitchen, making myself tea, I think unintentionally of an acquaintance who lives in Italy. Just an acquaintance because I have no idea about her plans and even less about her life. I wondered what would become of her. In less than five minutes, with tea in hand, I went down to the street and walked to my daughter's school. It was time to pick her up, but to my surprise I almost bumped into the acquaintance on the corner of the block from my house. What was she doing in New York? Where had Italy gone? After a casual greeting she told me that she had just arrived and that she would stay for three days, and without further details she left.

Troubled, I felt that during those seconds in the

kitchen I had penetrated an unknown dimension, like that afternoon, when I sensed that something bad was happening to Marta. What was wrong with me? According to my esoteric friend, it happened to me because I was hypersensitive. People like me are, according to some religions and beliefs, the most susceptible to diabolical possession. Was I possessed? Or would that premonition simply be a window to communicate and better understand the universe around me?

I thought I should learn to penetrate those incomprehensible boundaries. As an imposed exercise, I began to visualize everything from another angle. Flying over reality. I no longer saw the furniture fixed, stiff, motionless, but now I imagined it flying around me and not where my brain had placed them fifteen years ago. The same thing happened to me with people and even with my books. Now everything was relative, I went through life with the attitude of being contrary to the beings that cross our path and unconsciously we want to pigeonhole. Now I wanted to see them without labels, free, and although I am open to any plane where I can enrich the perception, for me nothing has a fixed place anymore, only my husband, Mauricio, who insists on staying there like an old, dusty, tired piece of furniture with nothing new to offer.

Since Mauricio returned from Rome, he has been different, not at all communicative, wandering aimlessly through the narrow streets of the neighborhood. He may have a thousand worries but only with time will he come to know. That is why I prefer not to deal with everyday problems. Well, he will get over it.

Seeing that pink flower, growing on the concrete at the entrance of the house, a flower that demands a little water, made me establish a comparison between water and solitude: The water necessary for every living being to live and the solitude necessary for the enrichment of the spirit. Those moments of solitude were vital to enter the new universe that was opening up before me.

That night the storm did not cease and after drinking a glass of warm milk, I fell asleep and dreamed of the barely known woman that crossed my path in NY. Through her gestures I saw an inferno, a fireball, and corpses strewn on the surrounding hill. In the same dream I mixed the barely known woman with Mauricio. How curious is the mind that, like in a cocktail shaker, intermingled the worries of the day.

The next day, while drinking coffee, I imagined that someone was shouting at me. Had I penetrated another dimension again? I remembered that the barely known woman had told me that at the end of the month she would be going to Florence on business, so I would look for her to calm and satisfy my curiosity.

The day of the trip arrived, and I almost missed the flight due to the traffic of this great city. Stepping on Italian soil and without stopping at the hotel, I went to her house. The servant was surprised. I asked him about Bethania, and he replied that it had just been a month since the tragedy: The plane in which she was flying had crashed into the highest hill in Rome. There was something I could not process, who did I see that afternoon? Wasn't she the one I almost bumped into in New York? And in the dreams, she pointed to the ball of fire and finally imagined that she was calling me, screaming. I still cannot understand.

On his last trip, Mauricio had traveled back on the same flight as her and never told me about any accident or how he had survived. In desperation, I read the newspapers. There were the names of the deceased: Bethania Alvarez, and among many others, Mauricio Velez. How then could I explain that month living with him? Will I be dead too?

Maria Gabriela Madrid

Maria Gabriela Madrid was born in Caracas, Venezuela. She studied Education at the Metropolitan University in Caracas, Venezuela, creative writing and English as a Second Language at Harvard University, Boston University and Columbia University.

Madrid obtained a Diploma and Honorable Mention for her participation in the Poetry and Narrative Competition XVII "Nicomedes Santa Cruz 2008" of the Institute of Peruvian Culture, Florida, U.S.A. The Mayor of Florida, Carlos Alvarez, presented the award.

In 2008 her story "Why?" aired on the program "Texas Matters" National Public Radio 89.1FM. Since 2008 her short story "Why?" has been broadcast during the holiday season.

In 2008, Maria Gabriela Madrid and Martha Curcio (now Martha Tavera) won the opportunity to participate in the "Luminarias March 14, 2009" Festival. Madrid and Curcio organized the group "Mandragora" that participated in the area of Literature in the Convention Center of San Antonio-Texas.

In 2009 the book of stories of her authorship "Entre los Surcos del Recuerdo "became part of the curriculum of the "Advanced IV Spanish" classes of Saint Mary's Hall School in San Antonio, Texas.

On April 25, 2009, Madrid participated with her short story "Las Tres Serpientes/The Three Snakes" at the "Literary Evening" of the Institute of Peruvian Culture in Miami-Florida.

On May 11, 2009, was the presentation of Maria Gabriela Madrid at Barnes and Nobles - San Pedro Crossing in San Antonio-Texas.

On May 23, 2009, Madrid was the guest of honor at the "Annual Dinner of the American Association of Teachers of Spanish and Portuguese (AATSP)" in San Antonio, Texas.

On June 27, 2009, Maria Gabriela Madrid presented her book "Entre los Surcos del Recuerdo" sponsored by the literary club "La Tertulia" at the public library "Brook Hollow Brach Library" in San Antonio, Texas.

On July 16, 2009, Maria Gabriela Madrid presented her book "Entre los Surcos del Recuerdo" in "El Buscón-Librería De Ocasión" at Trasnocho, Caracas-Venezuela.

On November 5, 2009, Madrid gave a lecture about "Venezuela and its culture" to the "Spanish Club" of Saint Mary's Hall in San Antonio, Texas.

On November 30, 2009, Madrid presented and commented its literary work to students of "Advanced Spanish" of Saint Mary's Hall in SA, TX.

In 2009 Maria Gabriela Madrid participated in "Lenguas Libres-Writers Block" at the Guadalupe Center for Arts and Culture (Guadalupe Cultural Arts Center).

On September 11, 2010, Maria Gabriela Madrid presented her book "Entre los Surcos del Recuerdo" at the Plaza de las Américas Community Center, Houston-Texas.

On February 20 and 21, 2010, Madrid participated and introduced her book "Entre los Surcos del Recuerdo" in the "Eighth Houston Hispanic Book Festival in Houston-Texas."

The Dance of the Shadows

On September 18, 2010, Maria Gabriela Madrid received a diploma for her participation with the short story "Las Tres Serpientes/The Three Snakes." in "Letras de la Frontera 2010".

In 2010 Madrid was interviewed by Amparo Ortíz from the program "Desde San Antonio" of the television network Univision, U.S.A.

On March 9, 2011, Maria Gabriela Madrid received the "Woman Writer of the Year 2010-2011" award by the representative of the Mayor of Houston, Anisse Parker, at the Norris Conference Center in Houston-Texas.

In 2011 Madrid received a diploma for her participation with the short story "La Herida Abierta/The Open Wound." in "Letras de la Frontera 2011."

On April 25, 2012, Maria Gabriela Madrid as guest author presented her short stories and poems at Barnes and Nobles in San Antonio-Texas.

In 2012 Madrid participated in the 32nd Anthology of the World Congress of Art and Culture (WAAC), affiliated to UNESCO, the United Nations Letters, Hispanic Union of Writers, IFLAC International Forum for Literature and Culture for Peace, Israel Association of Spanish Writers in Spanish Language, Argentine Society of Letters, Arts and Sciences, SALAC.

In 2013 Maria Gabriela Madrid received a diploma for her participation in "Letras de la Frontera 2013". Madrid participated with her short story "La virgin Roja/The Red Virgin" (based on the life of the philosopher Simon Weil).

On May 22, 2013, the guests Maria Gabriela Madrid and Carol Coffee Reposa presented their poems at Barnes & Nobles, San Antonio-Texas.

Maria Gabriela Madrid

In 2014 Maria Gabriela Madrid as author participated in the National Association of Hispanic Journalists 2014 (NCHJ). The books of his authorship "La Danza de las Sombras" (Spanish) and "The Poets' 'Web / La Telaraña del Poeta" (English and Spanish) were accepted to be part of the Carousel of the University of Texas-SA in the National Association of Hispanic Journalists 2014 (NAHJ).

Madrid participated in the anthology in Spanish "Poetas y Narradores 2008" of the Institute of Peruvian Culture, Miami, Florida.

Madrid participated in the anthology in Spanish "Poetas y Narradores 2009" of the Institute of Peruvian Culture, Miami, Florida.

Maria Gabriela Madrid participated in the anthology in English "Inkwell Echoes 2009-2010" of the Association of Poets of San Antonio (SAPA).

Maria Gabriela Madrid participated in the anthology in English "Inkwell Echoes 2010-2011" of the Association of Poets of San Antonio (SAPA).

Madrid participated in the bilingual anthologies "Voices de Mujeres / Voces de Mujeres (2009) published in the university Our Lady of the Lake University (OLLU).

Madrid edited with the collaboration of the poet and writer Pedro M. Madrid M (R.I.P) the books "Las Alas Perdidas" (2012) and "Arkontika" (2013). Both in Spanish at **amazon.com.**

Madrid translated and participated as an author in the bilingual anthology "Un Escorzo Tropical / A Tropical Foreshortening" 2014 by La Caverna, School of Creative Writing in Florida, U.S.A.

Madrid translated and participated as an author in the bilingual anthology "Muestrario de Ficciones Hispanoamericanas. Showcase of Latin American Fiction" of La Caverna, School of Creative Writing in Florida, U.S.A.

Madrid translated and participated as an author in the bilingual anthology "Vorágine Sensual / Sensual Vortex" from La Caverna, school of Creative Writing in Florida, U.S.A.

Madrid with the collaboration of the writer and Director José Díaz-Díaz edited the bilingual anthologies "Un escorzo tropical / A Tropical Foreshortening", "Muestrario de Ficciones Hispanoamericanas / Showcase of Latin American Fiction" and "Vorágine Sensual / Sensual Vortex" from La Caverna, School of Creative Writing, Florida, USA.

Madrid in 2015 compiled, edited and participated as author in the bilingual anthology "Voces Alzan Vuelo en el Reflejo de las Piedras Caídas / Voices Take Flight in the Reflection of the Fallen Stones" at amazon.com.

Madrid participated as author in the book of 2015 "El Gran Doctor de la Paz-Ernesto Kahan" compiled and edited by the writer Maria Cristina Azcona (Founder and President of WWPO-World Organization of Peace, Director of IFLAC in Latin America.

Madrid participated as one of the 40 authors interviewed in the book "Latina Authors and their Muses" (2015) winner of the first place in the International Book Festival as "Best Non-Fiction Book in English." Prologue from Leticia Gómez and Edited by Mayra Calvani. Publisher: Twilight Times Books, U.S.A.

On February 27, 2015 Madrid was the guest of honor and presented her books "La Danza de las Sombras", "The Poets'

Web / La Telaraña del Poeta" in the American Association of Teachers of Spanish and Portuguese (AATSP) in the A & M Arts and Culture Education Center in San Antonio, Texas.

In March 2015, Madrid translated into English the book "Un Encuentro Angelical / An Angelical Encounter" by television presenter Nancy Restrepo in Miami-Florida.

On March 28, 2015, Madrid participated as one of the judges of Poetry organized by the American Association of Teachers of Spanish and Portuguese (AATSP). Madrid also recited some poems and read two short stories of its authorship. The event was held at San Antonio College (SAC) in San Antonio, Texas.

On April 8, 2015, Madrid gave a lecture at Warren High School to a group of teachers from the North Side School District (NISD) in San Antonio, Texas.

On May 11, 2015, Madrid participated as a keynote speaker at the Induction Ceremony of William Taft High School in San Antonio, Texas.

In September 2015 the book "Latina Authors and Their Muses" was published by Mayra Calvani with a foreword by Leticia Gómez and printed by Twilight Times books where Maria Gabriela Madrid participated as one of the forty authors interviewed in the book.

The book "Latina Authors and Their Muses" won the first place as "Best Latin American Non-Fiction Book in English" at the International Festival of Latin Book Awards, U.S.A.

On September 15, Madrid finished the English translation of the book "Chenco" and wrote a comment about the artist's trajectory.

In September 2015, Madrid wrote an article about the trajectory of Alejandro Rosales-Lugo as an artist.

The Dance of the Shadows

In February 2016 Madrid presented her books "La Danza de las Sombras" and "The Poets' Web / La Telaraña del Poeta" at the Williams Uplift Preparatory School in Dallas, Texas.

On October 29, 2016, Maria Gabriela Madrid won First Place in "Conversando a través de la Poesía" at the Houston Festival of Books and Arts. Madrid won the First Prize and Diploma of recognition for her short story "Salomé."

On November 14 and 15, 2016, Madrid was a guest judge in the contest to declaim in Spanish of the elementary and secondary students of Cooper Academy in San Antonio-Texas.

On November 18 and 20, 2016, Madrid presented at the Kipp Youth High School the books "La Danza de las Sombras" and The Poets' Web / La Telaraña del Poeta" to high school students from different classrooms where they would study and analyzed the stories and poems as part of the school curriculum.

On March 29,2018 Maria Gabriela Madrid participated as a judge in the debate "Human Rights and Slavery XXI Century" in Kipp Youth Preparatory Highschool, San Antonio, Texas.

Beginning the school year 2016-2017, the books "La Danza de las Sombras" and "The Poets' Web / La Telaraña del Poeta" will be part of the curriculum of the superior Spanish classes at Kipp University Prep in San Antonio-Texas.

On May 1, 2010, Maria Gabriela Madrid was part of the "Welcome Committee of the American Latino Museum" at the Auditorium of the Capitol in Austin-Texas (Austin Welcoming Committee for the American Latino Museum at the State Capitol Auditorium).

Maria Gabriela Madrid was elected "Chief of Precinct 2014-2016" (Precinct Chair 2014-2016) for the Democratic Party.

Maria Gabriela Madrid

Madrid in 2013 became "Deputy Officer" (Democratic Party).

During the years of 2010 to 2012 Maria Gabriela Madrid was International Editor (Editora Internacional) of the magazine "Voices de la Luna" on paper and during 2012-2013 was one of the managers of the Virtual Magazine "Voices de la Luna" on Facebook.

During the years of 2010 to 2013 Maria Gabriela Madrid was a member of the board of directors of the magazine "Voices de la Luna."

Maria Gabriela Madrid's books: "La Danza de las Sombras" (Spanish), "The Poets' Web/La Telaraña del Poeta" (English and Spanish) and "Voices Take Flight In The Reflection of the Fallen Stones/ Voces Alzan Vuelo En El Reflejo de las Piedras Caídas" (English and Spanish) are at EBSCO Research Library.

Maria Gabriela Madrid currently resides in Bloomfield, Connecticut, U.S.A.

AWARDS:

1-On August 1, 2008 at the Consulate of Peru Maria Gabriela Madrid obtained "Diploma and Honorable Mention" for her short story "Pantalla Vacía/Empty Screen" in the Competition of "Poetry and Narrative XVII Nicomedes Santa Cruz 2008" of the Institute of Culture Peruvian, Florida, USA The poet and nominated Nobel Prize for Literature Luis Angel Casas read the minutes of the jury of which he was a member in the company of other notable poets and narrators. The Mayor of Florida Carlos Alvarez delivered the award.

2-In 2010 Maria Gabriela Madrid received the "Woman Writer of the Year 2010-2011" award in Houston, given by the representative of Houston Mayor Anisse Parker.

3-In 2016 Maria Gabriela Madrid won the First Place in "Conversando a la Poesía/Conversing with poetry" of the festival in Houston. Madrid won the First Prize for her short story "Salomé."

BOOKS:

1- "Entre los Surcos del Recuerdo" (Stories in Spanish) was included in the curriculum of the Advanced IV Spanish students at Saint Mary's Hall, SA, TX.

2- "La Danza de las Sombras" (Stories in Spanish) and "The Poets' Web / La Telaraña del Poeta" were included in the curriculum of the Advanced Spanish students at the Williams Uplift Preparatory School in Dallas-Texas.

3- "La Danza de las Sombras" and "The Poets' Web / La Telaraña del Poeta" (Bilingual Poems in Spanish and English) were included in the curriculum of the Advanced Spanish students at Kipp University Prep. in San Antonio, Texas.

4- Maria Gabriela Madrid's books: "La Danza de las Sombras" (Spanish), "The Poets' Web/La Telaraña del Poeta" (English and Spanish) and "Voices Take Flight In The Reflection of the Fallen Stones/ Voces Alzan Vuelo En El Reflejo de las Piedras Caídas" (English and Spanish) are at EBSCO Research Library.

ANTHOLOGIES:

1-2016 Bilingual Anthology "Vorágine Sensual / Sensual Vortex" La Caverna, Florida.

2-2015 Bilingual Anthology "Muestrario de Ficciones Hispanoamericanas/Showcase of Latin American Fiction" La Caverna, Florida.

3-2015 Bilingual Anthology "Voces Alzan Vuelo en el Reflejo

de las Piedras Caídas/ Voices Take Flight in the Reflection of the fallen Stones" Pukiyari Editores.

4-2014 Bilingual Anthology "Un Escorzo Tropical / A Tropical Foreshortening" La Caverna, Florida.

5-2012 Anthology in Various Languages "32 Anthology World Congress of Poets. Israel / 32ava Antología Congreso Mundial de Poetas.Israel" World Academy of Arts and Cultures (WAAC), United Nations (UN), UNESCO, IFLAC, SALAC, SIPEO, Editorial Brasego.

6-2010 Anthology in English "Inkwell Echoes 2010-2011" Association of Poets of San Antonio (SAPA)

7-2009 Anthology in English "Inkwell Echoes 2009-2010" Association of Poets of San Antonio (SAPA)

8-2009 Anthology in Spanish "Poetas y Narradores 2009" Institute of Peruvian Culture, Miami-Florida.

9-2009 Bilingual Anthology "Woman Voices / Voces de Mujeres 2009" Our Lady of the Lake University (OLLU), San Antonio-Texas.

10-2008 Anthology in Spanish "Poetas y Narradores 2008" Institute of Peruvian Culture, Miami-Florida.

11-Anthology in Spanish "El Gran Doctor de la Paz-Ernesto Kahan" compiled by Maria Cristina Azcona Founder and President of WWPO. Organization for World Peace. Director of IFLAC in Latin America. Published by Cook Communication, USA.

12-2015 Anthology in English "Latina Authors and Their Muses" Twilight Times Books. Winner of the first place as "Best Latin American Non-Fiction Book in English" at the

International Festival of Latin Book Awards, U.S.A. Compiled and Edited by Mayra Calvani.

13-2016 Anthology in Spanish "Expresiones de Sublimes Fantasías" del grupo Conversando a través de la poesía. Anthology of Short Stories and Poetry. Published by Lulu Press, Inc U.S.A.

JOURNALS:

1-2009 Poema "Silencio" published in the magazine "MALA" in Buenos Aires-Argentina.

2-2010 short story "Why" at "Voices de la Luna." Page 41.15 of June 2010. Volume 2, Number 4.

3-2010 short story "The Shinny Star" at "Voices de la Luna." Page 32. March 15, 2010. Volume 2, Number 4.

4-2010 short Story "Gasping for Air" Page 35. Poem without title in English and Spanish. "Voices de la Luna." Page 23. September 15, 2010. Volume 3. Number 1.

5-2011 Poem "Sueños / Dreams." Page 23. "Voices de la Luna." January 15, 2011. Vol. 3, Number 2.

6-2011 Poems "God/Dios." and "Rage/Rabia." Page 22. "Voices de la Luna." April 15, 2011. Volume 3, Number 3.

7-2011 Poem "Flores Salvajes/ Wildflowers." Page 23. "Voices de la Luna." July 15, 2011. Volume 3. Number 4.

8-2011 Poem "La Telaraña del Poeta / The Poet's Web." Page 23. "Voices de la Luna." October 15, 2011. Volume 4. Number 1.

9-2012 Poem "The Craft of a Poem /La Creación del Poema." Page 23. "Voices de la Luna." January 15, 2012. Volume 4. Number 2.

10-2012 Poem "Leonardo." Page 23. "Voices de la Luna." April 15, 2012. Volume 4. Number 3.

11-2012 Poem "Pensé que el Fuego / I Thought the Fire." Page 20. "Voices de la Luna."15 October 2012. Volume 5. Number 1.

12-2013 Poem "Sombras / Shadows." Page 28. "Voices de la Luna." April 15, 2013. Volume 5. Number 3.

13-2013 Poem "An Owls Cry." Page 27. "Voices de la Luna." July 15, 2013. Volume 5. Number 4.

INTERVIEWS (Newspaper, Radio, Television and internet)

1) 2009 Maria Gabriela Madrid was interviewed by Mayra Calvani for "Latino Books Examiner."

2) 2009 Madrid was interviewed by Álvaro Perez Capielo of "Diario Caracas" in Caracas, Venezuela.

3) Madrid was interviewed by Omar Lares for the column "Spirit" of the newspaper "El Universal" in Caracas-Venezuela.

4) 2009 Madrid was interviewed by Marta Colmenares for the Art and Literature section of "Diario Las Américas."

5) 2009 Maria Gabriela Madrid was interviewed by Rosalind Ortiz for the newspaper "North Central News" in San Antonio-Texas.

6) 2009 Madrid was interviewed by Dr. Santiago Dayli-Tolson for the virtual magazine "Café Labrapalabra."

7) 2009 Madrid was interviewed by Raquel Ludwig from "Prensa2pronóstico" in Caracas-Venezuela.

8) 2009 Madrid was interviewed by Carolina Branger on the "99.9 FM radio program" in Caracas-Venezuela.

9) 2010 Maria Gabriela Madrid was interviewed on the Houston radio program "Entérate con Ramón Rivera" 920 AM. From 2 to 3 in the afternoon.

10) 2010 Madrid was interviewed by Amparo Ortíz for the TV show "Desde San Antonio" from the Univisión network in San Antonio, Texas.

10) 2010 Madrid was interviewed by Alejandro Rosales Lugo for the "Eye of Cyclops" segment of the cultural section of the newspaper of Ciudad Victoria, Tamaulipas, Mexico.

12) In 2015 The writer and director of La Caverna, José Díaz-Díaz, School of Creative Writing presented the Anthology "Un Escorzo Tropical / A Tropical Foreshortening" where Madrid worked as co-editor and co-author in the radio cultural program "Cita con Caracol with Enrique Córdoba."

http://www.caracol1260.com/

ORGANIZATIONS:

Maria Gabriela Madrid has been linked to the following organizations:

1) Lifetime Member of the "World Congress of Poets" under "The World Academy of Arts and Culture" (WAAC). affiliated with UNESCO and registered in the United States of America.

2) Active member of the "Circulo de Escritores de Venezuela."

3) "Association of the Poets of San Antonio (San Antonio Poets Association) (SAPA)."

4) "Society of Latin and Hispanic Writers of San Antonio, Texas (Sociedad de Escritores Latinos e Hispanos de San Antonio-Texas) (SLHW)."